An Ounce of Death

Books by George T. Arnold

Old Mrs. Kimble's Mansion
Wyandotte Bound
The Heart Beneath the Badge
An Ounce of Death

For more information
visit: www.SpeakingVolumes.us

An Ounce of Death

George T. Arnold

SPEAKING VOLUMES, LLC
NAPLES, FLORIDA
2024

An Ounce of Death

ISBN 979-8-89022-264-0

To the authors and the screenwriters of western books and movies that have given me a lifetime of enjoyment and entertainment.

Chapter One

A deadly judgment
New Mexico 1889

A booming flash of gun muzzle light in the dimly lit barroom provided clear witness to the biggest bully in Santa Fe dropping ponderously to the floor, dead with his head butting up against an overflowing spittoon.

Cain "Kodiak" Booker unsuspectingly goaded the wrong man into a gun fight.

That piled-high-and-deep mountain of a man senselessly committed all of his twenty-eight years to sadistically pushing people around. The old folks swear he was born that way. Part of his nature, they claimed.

He came into the world huge and kept growing until he was an enormous three hundred fifty-five pounds stuffed onto an intimidating six-and-a-half-foot frame. Combined with his hard and fast savage behavior and a pathological craving for attention, it wasn't difficult to understand why Kodiak was a man to be feared.

Feared, as he wanted; not admired, as he wished.

Kodiak never bucked the odds, always choosing the targets of his abuse carefully. Farm boys. Older men whose reflexes had slowed. Drunks. Anyone who didn't appear to stand a chance against him.

The man he fatally misjudged this night looked like the perfect victim. Bib overalls. Plowing boots. Faded shirt. Barely old enough to order a drink.

But that young man's appearance was a carefully crafted disguise, intended to attract as little attention as possible wherever he went. He wanted no one who by chance had seen him in another town to recognize him as the fast draw, trick shot artist for the Traveling Sharp-shooters Exhibition.

Sure as hell fooled Kodiak. His ignorance of what that "hayseed" could do with a gun and an ounce of lead bought that giant a cheap pine coffin covered by six feet of dirt on Boot Hill. He was buried with shock carved so deep into his face, the undertaker couldn't put it right.

The shooter, Rance Cabell, feared he'd be going to jail. He couldn't understand why everyone in the saloon was cheering. Congratulating him. Pounding him on the back. Ordering him drinks.

He'd never killed a man before. Never even shot at one. The whole thing made him sick.

"Son," the bartender called out, "don'tcha know you just killed the meanest son of a bitch in town! You done us a favor, boy. Good riddance."

His remarks stirred up another round of cheers.

When the sheriff walked in a few minutes later to check out the situation, he took one look at the massive body slumped hideously on the floor and a long inspection of the shooter and said: "I don't believe it. A farm boy outdrew Kodiak!"

"Damn right," one of the witnesses shouted out.

"You shudda seen it, sheriff," another said. "Fastest I ever saw."

"Sheriff," Rance said almost pleadingly, "he didn't give me any choice. I was just standin' at the end of the bar, mindin' my own business. He came down, elbowed me out of his way, picked up my beer and drank the rest of it. Then he said, 'Whatcha gonna do about it, sodbuster?'

"I didn't say anything. I just moved to the other end of the bar and got myself another beer."

What Rance did not confess to the sheriff or to any other of the men listening was that he had been scared. Afraid from the moment Kodiak

2

pushed him aside until he himself somehow found the courage to draw his pistol and shoot that enormous bully. But was it courage or more simply a greater fear of death than of that merciless stranger? Regardless, Rance felt like a coward. He desperately wanted to back down. And tried to. Twice.

"Maybe, sheriff, I shudda just walked out of the saloon and away from trouble. But that overgrown tub of guts wouldn't let it go. He wanted to fist fight.

"So I said real loud right in front of everybody: 'Look, mister, I know you can kick my ass. All you'd have to do is fall on me, and there'd be nothin' left but a greasy spot. I'm not fightin' you.

"Then he said I'd better go for my gun 'cause he was gonna have his satisfaction one way or another. So, I said again loud enough for everybody to hear that I would admit he was better with a gun than me."

"What did he say or do then?" the sheriff wanted to know.

"He put his hand a few inches above his gun and said, 'If you don't draw first, then I will.'

"So, I drew, and so did he. I was faster.

"But I swear I never wanted to kill him. Gal dammit, I didn't even know him. I just got into town. Don't know anybody here."

"Where'd you learn to draw so fast?" the sheriff asked.

"I'm a trick shot artist. But all I've ever shot before were bottles and cans and other targets."

"Are you part of that exhibition group that's going to put on a show here in a couple of days?"

"Yessir, I am."

"Then why are you dressed like a farmer?"

"To keep me from being recognized. When people learn I do exhibition shootin' for a livin', they pester the hell out of me to show off for them. Worse, I'm always worried somebody who wants to build his reputation with a gun will force me into a fight. Like this guy did tonight. Only I guess he figured he was pickin' on a farm boy."

"You can count on that," the sheriff said. "If he'd known who you are, he'd been buyin' you drinks, not bullyin' you.

"By the way, let me see your pistol, if you don't mind. I'm bettin' it's one of those new double-action revolvers that you don't have to cock before you pull the trigger."

"That's right, sir," Rance said, handing over his weapon to give the sheriff a good look.

"Because I'm a fast-draw artist, I prefer the Colt 1877 Thunderer because all you have to do is draw and pull the trigger. Obviously, that's faster than havin' to cock the hammer and then squeeze the trigger. The trigger is a little stiffer because it's doin' two actions, but you get used to that. Some say the single-action revolver is more accurate because the trigger squeeze is lighter, but I haven't found that to be the case."

"Well, I see what you mean, son. But for us old-timers accustomed to single-action guns, your pistol would take a mighty big adjustment."

"Now, you better walk with me. Best to getcha outta here. Only way to stop these drunks you impressed from keepin' you up all night. Got a place to stay, do you?"

"No sir, sheriff. Like I said, I just got into town right before I went into the saloon for a drink. Wished now I'da gone to a hotel and straight to bed."

"I got an idea, if it suits you, son. If you don't mind the bars on the windows, I can putcha up in my jail for the night. I'm stayin' there myself to look after a couple of prisoners. I keep clean sheets and blankets on the beds, and the mattresses ain't a whole lot worse than them at the hotel."

"Appreciate that, sheriff. But I don't know how much sleep I'll be gettin'. I can't believe I just ended the life of another human bein'—no matter how sorry of a life that bully had been livin'. I'm afraid I'm feelin' guilty about it."

"Well, don't, boy. If you hadn't killed him, you'd be dead yourself. It was a plain case of self defense. And, believe me, I've seen enough of them to know."

"Yessir, sheriff. But how do I live with it? Will God ever forgive me?

"I mean, you've been a lawman for a long time. How did you find peace with havin' to kill another person?"

"Well, son, believe it or not, my reaction to shootin' my first outlaw was much the same as yours. It bothered me to the point that I went to see an old preacher in a town where I grew up, not far from here. He set me straight by explainin' that killin' had long been part of what he called 'the human condition' ever since Cain murdered Abel. Not a stranger or a bad man, but his own brother.

"Then he reasoned that most people who had ever lived were generally well-meanin' folk who meant to exist in peace with their fellow man. But there also were evil people who stole, robbed, cheated, and even murdered. Someone has to protect the innocent and others who can't save themselves. He told me that as a lawman, I was one of those protectors.

"So, Rance, my experience in wearin' a badge more than twenty years leads me to tell you to look at the killin' of Kodiak this way: Every time it bothers your conscience, just think of how many other innocent people's lives you saved tonight by keepin' Kodiak from killin' them."

Rance felt some immediate relief from the sheriff's words, but he knew only time would help him reconcile everything. He did appreciate, however, the sheriff's willingness to share his personal story to point the way forward for him. He had a feeling he'd remember this lawman for the rest of his life. But all he knew him by was "sheriff."

"By the way, I know you're the sheriff, but I don't know your name."

"Well, I do have one, but most people just call me sheriff. My ma put down Randolph Mercer on my birth certificate. So, call me Randolph, if you like. But for God's sake, don't use Randy. Sounds like a name for a kid who still pisses his drawers."

Chapter Two

Big with a gun

Rance Cabell was no gunslinger, but it wasn't too far fetched to claim he'd cut his teeth on firearms. His daddy, Patterson, bought, sold, and repaired them for a living on the first floor of his store in downtown Mabscott, Kansas. He and his wife, Fanny, lived upstairs with their two sons and a daughter.

Everybody in the family could accurately shoot any weapon that had a trigger. Patterson and Fanny figured if their kids were going to grow up with guns everywhere in the building, they'd better gain some early respect for them.

So, stressing safety first, Patterson slowly and carefully taught his children everything he thought they needed to know. When the youngest, Taylor, reached the age of ten, Patterson quit locking his stock of merchandize away. By then, the children's education was complete.

Rance's older brother, Tyrone, took to the business right away and followed his father around like his shadow. He loved figuring out the mechanics of guns, how to take them apart, repair them, and put them back together. The whole family took for granted Tyrone would some-day take over the shop after his dad retired.

Taylor was small and delicate looking at thirteen years of age, but when she was on her own at home or walking around Mabscott by her-self, she was known to conceal a little derringer on her person. Any frisky boy trying to put his hands where they didn't belong would back off right fast when his fingers felt cold, hard metal instead of warm, soft skin.

But she didn't share her father's or her brothers' interest in weapons, other than for personal protection.

Besides, Taylor was already a beauty. And she knew it. Her mirror did not lie. In her reflection, she approved of her long blond hair, large green eyes, and maturing body. So did all the boys of her acquaintance. Her mother figured Taylor's maiden status wouldn't last past her sixteenth birthday.

Rance was the only one of their children Patterson and Fanny worried about for being born into such a dangerous business. He liked weapons of all kinds a little too much. He spent all the time they'd let him out behind the house at the firing range customers used to try out the pistols, rifles, and shotguns before they bought them. Patterson used the range every day to make sure his repairs were perfect.

Rance practiced his quick draw every chance he could, sneaking away from school and his chores, drawing and firing until his right hand and fingers ached. He had the talent right off. By the time he was fourteen, he was fast and deadly—if you could use that term for killing tin cans and bottles. And he was itching for his parents' permission to let him enter the shooting contests so popular in their part of the country.

He was so good his parents worried the reputation he would surely earn very quickly might lead to him being challenged by more than sharpshooters competing for money. Gunslingers out to build their own reputation could be eager to make Rance another notch on their pistol handle.

Nevertheless, Rance was eager to be known for his fast draw and deadly accuracy. Otherwise, if it weren't for his boyish good looks, he'd hardly be noticed—much less be respected and admired. He was only five-feet five-inches tall on tiptoe and weighed maybe a hundred and thirty pounds. Soaking wet.

When he was sixteen and hadn't grown a fraction in two years, he reluctantly accepted his size, making him even more determined to impress men with his prowess with guns. He was also mindful that he could use his skills and his showmanship to attract pretty females. After guns, the ladies took priority in his ambitions.

He was also motivated to offset his small stature that made him a target of bullies from his first day of school until his classmates discovered he could work wonders with a pistol.

Rance learned when he was young what it was to be afraid. Not of things grown ups feared like not having enough money to provide for their families, or disease, or the criminal element that existed in every Western town. Rance had been afraid every day in elementary school of being bullied, and he hated the shame and embarrassment that caused him.

He feared Bruno Buttus in particular. Bruno was as oversized as Rance was undersized when they were twelve-year-old elementary school kids. Rance could never quite figure out why Bruno was so mean. Maybe he was as self-conscious about his looks as Rance was about his size.

Bruno was all torso balanced awkwardly on skinny legs, sort of like an egg atop two toothpicks. He had a nose so upturned it looked piggish, and his eyes were as close together as a possum's. Rance sometimes wondered if people could see though Bruno's nose straight into his brain at the same time they were looking into his eyes.

Girls avoided Bruno, and the only friends he had among the boys were hangers-on who thought they looked tough merely because of their association with the biggest bully in school.

Rance was a natural target for Bruno and his bunch. Physically, he stood no chance against him, and Bruno—who was not as stupid as he was ugly—figured out very quickly how to get under Rance's skin.

"Well, here comes the pygmy," Bruno would call out loudly whenever he spotted Rance walking into the crowded classroom as school was beginning or after students were returning from recess. "How could a Goliath mommy produce such a runt of a boy?" he would laugh while encouraging his friends to join in the ridicule.

Rance was genuinely afraid of Bruno because the few times he had tried to push back, Bruno had shoved him to the ground, embarrassing him in front of the other students. It was particularly humiliating for all the girls to be glancing down at him as he picked himself up. It brought bitter tears of anger and hatred to his eyes. He fantasized about bringing one of his father's guns to school and shooting that overgrown brute right in front of all the other students.

His family was not much help. He never brought up the subject of bullying, but one time when he hit his face on a desk as he was being pushed over, he suffered a small cut and a very noticeable bruise beneath his left eye. Fanny and Patterson obviously were curious, and despite Rance's reticence, they demanded he tell them what happened to him.

Fanny then wanted to have a joint meeting with Bruno's parents and the teacher. The idea mortified Rance.

"You can't do that, mother," Tyrone piped up. "Everyone in school will think Rance is a coward hidin' behind his mother's skirts. Rance needs to take care of this himself."

"Easy for you to say, Tyrone," Rance said bitterly in a raised voice. "You're big for your age, so nobody's ever picked on you. You don't know how it feels."

"Then what do you suggest, Tyrone? Patterson?" Fanny persisted.

Patterson had the solution, with which Tyrone totally agreed. "Son, the only way to handle a bully is to stand up to him. If you keep runnin' from him, he'll never stop pickin' on you."

"How do I do that, dad?" Rance responded.

"Here's how," Patterson said without hesitation. "The next time he starts in on you, haul off and punch him as hard as you can right in his piggy nose. That will surprise him, especially if his nose bleeds. Then he'll move on to someone else who hasn't stood up to him."

Fanny was totally opposed, and for good reason. Rance stood no chance in a fist fight against that tyrant.

Rance wasn't too keen on the idea either, but he resolved to give it a try, even though just thinking about it made him tremble. He did not have to wait long to put his dad's solution to the test. Sure enough, Bruno needled him again, insulting not only Rance but also his "gigantic" mother.

Rance shocked Bruno by socking him on the nose as hard as he could. Bruno was momentarily stunned but quickly responded, not by retreating as Patterson and Tyrone predicted but by beating the absolute hell out of Rance, bloodying his nose, busting his mouth, and dirtying his clothes by knocking him all over the playground.

So much for his family's advice.

The teacher called for the meeting Fanny had proposed the night before. Rance, however, had another idea if he could trick Bruno into falling for it. He would have to appeal to Bruno's pride because Rance was going to dare him in front of all his gang to come to his house before his parents met there.

"I've got another way of fightin' you besides using fists," Rance challenged.

"That's stupid," Bruno argued. "How can you fight without usin' your hands? Are you tellin' me you want to get into an ass-kickin' contest?" he laughed, as if he had said the funniest thing anyone had ever heard.

But he took the challenge and agreed to come. Rance was ready, leading Bruno into the back yard unseen by anyone else other than four of his hangers-on. The back yard was Rance's father's shooting range. And Rance was wearing a holster containing a small pistol, the same one he had been using for a couple of years when he practiced shooting.

About twenty feet from where the boys stood were six glass jars sitting atop fence posts.

Bruno and his followers didn't know what Rance was up to, but it did occur to them that Rance might shoot Bruno in retaliation for the beating the day before.

"Bruno, you know and so does everybody else that because of our size difference, you can beat the crap out of me anytime you want. But I'm gonna show you why you better not try it again. There are more ways to fight than with fists, and I am gonna demonstrate with six pieces of lead that weigh less than an ounce each why I can put an end to you pickin' on me."

"An ounce!" Bruno scoffed. "You must be nuts."

"Oh, yeah. Just watch this." And without any fanfare or bragging, Rance did a quick draw with his pistol and shot all six of those glass jars off their posts in less than five seconds.

While Bruno and his cohorts were staring wide-eyed, open-mouthed and speechless, Rance twirled the pistol expertly back into its holster.

That display of Rance's talent with a deadly weapon ended any need for future intervention by parents or school officials. Rance was now the giant of the elementary school.

* * *

Rance's mother offered living proof that women taller than Rance would not automatically be put off by his size. Fanny stood a good three inches above her five-foot seven-inch husband, and it didn't seem to bother him. Fact is, Rance had already figured what he'd say if he married someone taller. He'd borrow the line his dad always used: "I wanted a wife I could look up to."

Truth is, Patterson believed Fanny's size helped him to marry above his class. He came from a family of farmers and merchants; she, from bankers, lawyers, and doctors. She was pretty, had a good figure, an intelligent sense of humor, and an infectious laugh. But few suitors. Most men's egos kept them from marrying a woman who towered over them. Didn't bother Patterson one whit, and that endeared him to Fanny and to her family.

Like his father, Rance was nice looking. Both had round faces, friendly hazel eyes, a mop of unruly curly hair, and a mischievous smile that others found intriguing.

Rance, however, did not look the least little bit like his older brother. Physically, Tyrone didn't favor anyone else in the family. At six-feet-one-inch, he was taller than his mother, but his face and size must have been influenced by an ancestor many generations back. He had deep set dark eyes, a beefy body, and bushy hair growing everywhere—his arms, legs, chest, shoulders, back, and even in his ears. His siblings teased him mercilessly, telling him he looked as if he needed to be mowed.

The Cabells may not have been the most conventional family in Mabscott, but as different as they were in size and in looks, they were happy. They held hands and offered a prayer of thanks before every meal, faithfully attended church every Wednesday evening and Sunday, and prayed individually on their knees before getting into bed at night.

The Cabell family lived in a home with an abundance of good humor and love.

Chapter Three

Competitive shooter

Rance pestered his parents for months before his sixteenth birthday, repeating endlessly that all he wanted was their permission and support to become a competitive shooter. That was against Patterson's and Fanny's better judgment, but they admitted to each other Rance was going to do it even if he had to sneak away.

So, they compromised. The two stipulations for their backing were that he combine shooting with his studies until he graduated from high school, and Rance could not compete anywhere or in any contest without his father being present.

Rance willingly agreed. He wouldn't admit it, but the thought of venturing out on his own was intimidating. He'd never been anywhere, and he was concerned he would not be taken seriously by older competitors or perhaps not even allowed to compete without a parent being present and giving consent.

"They may not think you're old enough, son, but if need be, I can register your name without them knowin' until shootin' time it was for you and not me. Once they see you shoot, they'll know the crowd will raise hell if they don't let you continue."

Locally, the only matches available were turkey shoots at town and county fairs where people competed with rifles. Rance was not interested. He could use a rifle well enough to shoot game to help provide meat for his family's table, but beyond that he didn't care for that weapon.

He had trained himself to draw fast and shoot accurately with a pistol. To do that better than anyone else was his only goal.

So, his dad took him by train to notorious Dodge City, where men didn't feel completely dressed without a holster and pistol strapped around their waist. Patterson made certain Rance was similarly outfitted, but only at the shooting matches.

Most men, and some boys Rance's age and even younger, competed in the rifle matches. Virtually all males of a certain age were hunters, so no one was the least bit surprised to see anyone from grandpas to grandsons showing up with their rifles.

However, Rance stood out as the only boy in the pistol competition. To say he was given no respect at the outset would be an understatement. Some of the men even complained to the judges that a boy had no business testing himself against them. What they did not say out loud was how embarrassing, even humiliating, it would be to be beaten by a fuzz-faced kid.

Rance's match was against some of the best shots in the territory. Most were exhibition shooters; a few were gunslingers, or shootists as they also were known, enjoying putting their deadly artistry with a pistol on display against objects that couldn't shoot back. The targets were six glass jars placed twenty feet away and moved in increments of five feet until only the winner was standing alone.

Rance impressed everyone by making it to the final round with only three shooters left. He lost. But not by much. He came in second when the sweaty palm of his gun hand slipped and caused him to miss the last one of six jars.

"It got so hot, sweat ran down my arm and hand and made the grip slippery, Dad. Can you do somethin' to keep the handle from gettin' wet?"

"Well, I can't stop the sweat, but I know how to keep moisture from bein' a factor."

Before the next match, his father replaced the smooth wooden handle with thicker pieces of ivory with scallops carved into them, forming a rough grip. Not sharp enough to cut Rance's hand, but with enough edges to overcome sweat, rain, blood, or any other kind of wetness.

Rance rarely lost again, gaining respect the more he competed. Although others could shoot as accurately, no one could draw and shoot faster. He was also making some enemies, jealous that he was better than they were and eager to see him vanish.

Unaware, Rance carried on and his reputation grew. He moved up to stronger competitions in bigger cities where he shot for money, making enough to pay his and his father's expenses and to allow the Cabells to live comfortably when added to what Patterson and Tyrone could bring in at the store, which Tyrone ran in his father's frequent absences while traveling with Rance.

Rance's big break came when he was nineteen. That's when he met up with a man remarkably unlike any other he had ever known.

Chapter Four

Rance turns professional

Rance became a full-time professional exhibition shooter when he finished school and was almost nineteen. By that time, he had been participating in shooting contests tor two years throughout several western states and territories and was getting to be well known.

His expanding reputation caught the eye of a former college professor from the East who had ventured West looking for a way to get rich. His salary for teaching underclassmen English composition at swanky Swarthmore College in Pennsylvania did not allow him to live in the style to which he wanted to become accustomed.

Dr. Percy Merryweather Livingston Hardcastle IV had a booming voice, knew practically every word in the dictionary, and could talk a polar bear out of its winter coat.

He was a natural showman, and to make himself stand out, he dressed like an upperclass blue-blood from some snooty family in New York City: double-breasted coats of fine wool over light-colored waistcoats with lapels, white linen shirts, and striped trousers. All tailor-made, of course. His favorite hats were a black silk top hat and a black Homburg.

He looked as if he was born to wear such outfits, and those clothes, combined with his six-foot height, slim physique, clean-shaven face, light skin, and reasonably handsome face made the professor an attraction unto himself.

"I'm never going to get rich pontificating on the powers of the spoken and written word in front of a bunch of overprivileged freshmen from wealthy families," he told his closest colleagues when he resigned. "I would impress them infinitely more if I had as much money as their parents."

All he needed was a show.

He figured he could promote the healing qualities of snake oil, peddle pots and pans, and sell bolts of cloth for dressmaking and other uses to small general stores in all the little western towns. And for good measure, he also carried an official-looking license that signified he could legally perform weddings, preside at funerals, and when hard up enough, preach a sermon that would literally scare the hell right out of sinners—at least for a few days.

But as useful as these sidelines could be, Dr. Percy, as he chose to be called, needed a show that would be so spectacular it could draw large crowds of everyday folks to whom he could hawk his other products and services.

A year or so after coming west and barely making enough profit to get by, Dr. Percy happened to be in a town with posters in storefront windows promoting a sharpshooting contest.

"Going to see those sharpshooters, mister?" a freckle-faced little boy carrying a fishing pole and a bucket of worms asked when Dr. Percy kept staring at the poster.

"I'm thinking about it, my good lad. Have you seen them perform?"

"No, sir."

"How come?"

"Don't got the fifty cents to get in."

"Well, you do now, young man. So, if your parents won't mind, come along with me. I'd like to know what you think of the performance after you've seen it."

Dr. Percy and his new friend attended, and halfway through the show, Dr. Percy was so impressed he got hit by one of those bolt-of-lightning inspirations. Added to the excitement he could see in Jody, his companion, and in the adults as well, Dr. Percy made up his mind.

"By damn, I'm going to put together a team of sharpshooters and tour the West, charging admission and offering cash prizes to any of the locals who want to test their skills against one or more of my team members. Of course, the locals will have to put up a fee to qualify," he chuckled. "But I'll give them a three-to-one incentive and match all side bets to boot."

Dr. Percy's concept didn't stop there. Oh, no. Still too common-place. Other teams of shooters were already doing the same thing. A bottle of Hennessy cognac brought on a vision. He would search far and wide until he could find a diverse range of team members, prefer-ably one white man hardly older than a boy, an attractive female, and perhaps an Indian or an Asian or a Black man.

But where to find such an eclectic group?

Dr. Percy already had settled on Rance, and when he heard Annie Oakley had a cousin who was almost as good a shooter as her famous relative, he enlisted Abigail "Abby" Mosey, the same birth name Annie had before changing it to Oakley. Abby and Annie were related on their fathers' side of the family. Abby followed Annie's example with the name change, taking advantage of her relative's established popularity. Didn't hurt that Abby was also prettier than Annie.

Finding the third member was challenging. Because black men were not allowed to have firearms back when they were enslaved, the pickings were slim. Dr. Percy approached several black men who had fought as youngsters in the Civil War, but none had been given the opportunity to achieve sharpshooter status. But Dr. Percy considered finding that third member imperative. He would not give up until he achieved his goal.

Chapter Five

Rance and Abby impress each other

Rance had mixed feelings about joining Dr. Percy's Traveling Sharp-shooters Exhibition. Mostly he was excited and looking forward to the adventure of traveling all over the West and perhaps even to the East and eventually overseas, if the show became popular enough.

But he also had to admit to being a little fearful—something he was not about to share with family members, Dr. Percy, or anyone else. Rance had too much pride for that. He was anxious about breaking out on his own away from home, the security of his parents, siblings, friends, church, and the community in which he'd always felt so comfortable.

Rance barely knew Dr. Percy and had not yet met Abby Oakley or the third member Dr. Percy was trying to find to round out the team. Although many other nineteen-year-old men in the West had left home at an earlier age, Rance had led a sheltered life. For the first time, his dad would not be traveling with him.

When Rance got off the train in St. Louis, where the Traveling Sharpshooters Exhibition was to put on its first show, he was met by a beaming Dr. Percy and a brown-haired woman dressed in buckskin with fringe up and down each arm and around the bottom of her skirt.

She stood slightly behind Dr. Percy, leaving the greeting and introductions up to him. But, surely, Rance thought, this little woman who looked to be in her early twenties, could not be Abby Oakley. She was not more than five feet tall. And then Rance remembered from his reading about her famous cousin that Annie herself was very small.

"Welcome, my boy! Welcome indeed!" Dr. Percy said loudly, pumping Rance's hand as if he were greeting his best friend of a lifetime. Dr. Percy, Rance discovered at their first meeting some time ago, was always a showman, attracting attention to himself and to everyone else associated with him.

"You're looking fit and ready to show the world what you've got, Rance. And let me introduce the woman you will be dazzling the crowds with. May I present Miss Abby Oakley."

Rance noticed immediately that Abby, his senior by at least five years, was right pretty and presented a nice figure. He liked what he saw, but his inexperience with grown women was so meager, all he could do was blush slightly and say hello. In contrast, Abby seemed totally uninhibited, taking Rance by the hand and saying, "Looking forward to seeing you handle your pistol. From what Dr. Percy tells me, you're about as good with it as I am with a rifle."

Rance just smiled. He didn't want to appear either lacking in confidence or overconfident, so he didn't respond to what seemed to be more than a rhetorical question.

Dr. Percy had a buggy waiting to take the quarter-mile trip to the Emerald Hotel, which was within walking distance of the showgrounds where his team would join others in a fair featuring all kinds of exhibitions, none of which, thankfully, would be another competing gun show.

After settling into their rooms and hastily eating a light lunch, the three took their equipment by buggy to the site where they would show off their skills. Dr. Percy wanted to run through the routine he had carefully planned, and he also wanted his two stars to see each other in action.

For now, they were his only two team members. Dr. Percy was still trying to find an Indian, an Asian, or a Black sharpshooter to fill the third slot in what would surely be the most universal group traveling the West.

Abby took her turn first. Using her Winchester 1873 44-40 caliber rifle, she shot a variety of targets ranging from glass bottles to silver-dollar-size pieces of metal. Saving her best trick for last, she shot a cigar from Dr. Percy's clinched teeth from a range of about twenty-five feet.

During a half-hour of practice, she missed not a single shot.

Mightily impressed watching her go through her paces, Rance wondered how she could be so good, and yet not be anywhere near as well known as her famous cousin. Why wasn't she touring the entire United States and Europe as Annie was? He posed the question to Dr. Percy.

"For a very simple reason, my boy," Dr. Percy whispered. "Abby can shoot the balls off a gnat at fifty paces. She is every bit as good a shot as Annie. But the difference—and it is huge—is Abby can shoot accurately only when her body is stationary.

"Annie can shoot while atop a galloping horse, swinging from a trapeze bar, riding a bicycle, and she can even shoot backward holding a rifle over her shoulder while looking into a mirror or a shiny knife blade. Those are skills our Abby does not possess."

Abby was equally impressed watching Rance go through his routine. He started each phase with a blazing fast draw, knocking over cans, bottles, and other objects from a variety of distances. When Dr. Percy produced a spinning wheel with glass bulbs, Rance hit every one as fast as he could pull the trigger.

Then he surprised and delighted Dr. Percy and impressed Abby with his latest skill he had been practicing for a couple of years but had never displayed in public. He drew his pistol while turning sideways and wrapping his gun arm around his back to shoot objects from his left side. He knew crowds would love this trick, and he hoped they would not notice that he cut the distance and also made the target a mite bigger.

As they left the exhibition area, Dr. Percy had dollar signs in his eyes. He was already counting the money his little show was going to rake in. All that was left was to display to Rance and Abby the fancy outfits he had tailor-made for them.

"Nobody's performers anywhere are going to look more resplendent than mine," he boasted to Abby and Rance.

"I think 'gaudy' might be a more accurate description," Abby joked.

Undeterred, Dr. Percy insisted his judgment was sound. "Showmanship, my dear lady. Showmanship. Those sparkling outfits look like money in the bank to me."

Chapter Six

Wide awake and thinking

At 2 a.m. Rance was still wide awake, only twelve hours before he would have to make his debut performance before not only Dr. Percy and Abby but also a crowd of strangers whose expectations would be high because of the vastly inflated promises from the carnival-like posters tacked up all over town.

Not to mention that Dr. Percy had missed no opportunities, large or small, to fascinate the locals with his oratory from the bar rooms to the barber shops with extravagant claims about the skills of his sharpshooters. Dr. Percy did not seem at all apprehensive about the opening performance, and, as far as Rance could tell, neither did Abby.

He believed he had Dr. Percy figured out, but Abby puzzled him. Truth was that on the first day they met and practiced together, he felt awed by her. She was not in the least bit shy. She seemed worlds ahead of him in life experiences and sophistication.

Dr. Percy had told him some background information on Abby, just as he had informed her about the young man with whom she would be performing. Shockingly—at least shocking to Rance—Abby had been married and divorced. Divorce was rare, and in most cases was not approved. It could even make some women social outcasts.

Maybe that's why she seemed to feel so at ease around men. She was married at seventeen and divorced at twenty-two. To Rance, who was still a virgin at nineteen, Abby already knew everything about romance and sex. That made him eager to find out if she saw him as something of a younger brother to be looked out for, or if she would accept him as a man.

"Damn," Rance mumbled to himself, "I'm already fallin' for her when what I need most right now is some sleep and a way to control my nervousness about the exhibition."

Abby, too, was still awake in her room a couple of doors down the hall. Unlike Rance, she was not worried about her performance. She had supreme confidence in her abilities to shoot accurately in front of any crowd, large or small. She knew both her strengths and her weaknesses. She accepted the fact that she would never have the skills of her famous older cousin. They liked each other, but they were not close. They knew each other only from the times their families had visited, especially when they were young.

Abby had watched Annie perform enough to recognize why Annie had become famous in the United States and in Europe while Abby herself was just starting her first tour for a small, and as yet unknown, group called the Traveling Sharpshooters Exhibition. Abby knew she was as accurate with any rifle as Annie, but as Dr. Percy informed Rance, she had to be standing still to hit her targets. She could please paying customers in the West, but she never would be performing before European royalty.

However, that was not her goal. What she wanted was to make as much money as she possibly could. Being financially independent was hard enough for a man. Damned hard for a woman of ambition. She had no interest in being married again; she liked being her own boss too much for that. And she loathed the idea of birthing babies. She was fond of them and enjoyed being around them—just so long as they belonged to other women.

As far as Rance was concerned, she was withholding judgment until she got to know him better. What she did know was he was one hell of a shot and performer. It was obvious to her Rance also knew he was good but that he had no idea he was so good that one day he might find himself being part of a show like Annie's.

Otherwise, he no doubt was shy, especially around women he found attractive, as she was sure he had already considered her to be. But he had no clue how to talk with women, much less how to romance them.

"Maybe I can teach him a few things." The mischievous thought made her smile.

"Just maybe."

Meanwhile, Dr. Percy was sleeping soundly in another room on the same floor of the Emerald Hotel. The fact that he rarely, if ever, worried about anything—combined with several drinks of fine Hennessy cognac—brought on a deep slumber.

Of course, he had overpromised in his posters and in his bragging all over town. But that was simply show biz. People expected it. It made them all the more eager to show up and spend their money.

All of his blather, Rance's and Abby's glittering costumes, the noise of the shooting, and the smell of gun powder would help mislead the spectators into thinking they were seeing something grander than it actually was. Dr. Percy did not get to be Dr. Percy by some fortunate accident. He earned his Ph.D. degree with intelligence and ambition. His attractive face and physique were gifts of Nature and a select group of genes from equally blessed ancestors.

His biggest driving force—his lust for money—came from his overwhelming desire to live a life of luxury among the elites back East and the big cattle and oil families in the West.

He had no doubt he would achieve his goal. It was just a matter of when.

Chapter Seven

Neither rain, nor thunder, nor lightning . . .

Thunder boomed so deafeningly loud and deep that it rattled the windows and vibrated the entire four-story Emerald Hotel, startling guests awake just before daybreak.

To Rance, it sounded as if planets were colliding and made him even more apprehensive about what he would have to face in just a few hours. He half wished the raging storm would lead to a postponement because even if the rain stopped, at best there would be less light, restricting his vision and affecting his aim.

Abby wasn't intimidated by the noise or the lightning or the rain. She had lived through tornadoes in Oklahoma. But she did give the Weather Gods a good cussing for the mess the moisture and humidity would make of her hair and the dulling effect it would have on her outfit, which would sparkle only in good sunlight.

Dr. Percy saw visions of dollar bills sprouting wings and riding the winds as fast and as far away from him as they could go.

Not exactly the beginning he had envisioned for the Traveling Sharpshooters Exhibition.

The show was scheduled for 2 p.m., and at 7 a.m. the storm showed no signs of letting up. Abby just said "the hell with it" and went back to bed. She pulled the covers up to her chin, feeling toasty all over and actually enjoying the sound of the rain attacking the roof and the windows. Great sleeping weather for her. She didn't know exactly why; she had always liked it, even when she was a child.

Rance tried to distract himself by writing individual letters to his dad, his mother, Tyrone, and Taylor. "Now what?" he asked himself, wishing he had a good book to read. Wishing even more that he liked to read.

Dr. Percy busied himself seeking reassurance from anybody and everybody gathered in the breakfast room and in the lobby, hoping someone would convince him the rain would let up soon. Most people said, more or less in these words: "Damned if I know. Your guess is as good as mine."

However, one old fella with a neat white beard and a look of confidence held out hope to Dr. Percy. "My rheumatiz has been lettin' up for almost an hour. Tells me the weather is gonna clear in no time. Sure sign, young fella. Never fails me."

Dr. Percy picked up the bill and paid for the man's breakfast. He was the only one who offered hope—and he turned out to be right. By 10 a.m., the dark clouds had moved on, the wind had died down, and sunlight was breaking out all over.

The show would go on!

* * *

By noon, men, women, and children of all ages began filling the fairgrounds, heading straight for the refreshments: roasted corn, German funnel cakes, hot dogs and other sausages, lemonade, and a wide assortment of candies.

The mood was festive, and everybody from the toddlers to the grannies and grandpas were enjoying a brief time away from their everyday toils and boredom. The little boys in particular couldn't wait to see the sharpshooters, and the little girls were thrilled to hear one of them was a woman.

Rance and Abby were covered hat to boots in outfits in which Dr. Percy took particular pride. Rance's off-white jacket and pants were embroidered in a western theme of colorful bucking broncos, woolly headed bisons, horseshoes, pistols, and multi-stem cacti—or cactuses, as the locals referred to them. His boots were a deep brown with an ivory-handle pistol design on the outside of each.

Abby's skirt and vest also were off white and loaded with sequins and spangles of all colors, making her sparkle anew with every breaking ray of sunshine. Her scarf was a deep scarlet, as were her western boots with fringe running from top to bottom in the back.

When she saw the audience's reaction to their "gaudy" outfits, Abby was sorry she doubted Dr. Percy's judgment.

She mentioned it to Rance. "You know, Rance, he's been right so far about everything. I think we can put aside any doubts we've had and trust his judgment."

"I always have," Rance said with a mild scolding tone and a laugh. "He's the smartest man I've ever run across. Look, if these outfits and Dr. Percy's showmanship get the crowd on our side before we've fired the first shot, we've got it made."

Predictably, Dr. Percy had on his rich man's formal looking coat and trousers. As a finishing touch, he had added two affectations: a long cigarette holder and a monocle that never failed to fascinate western folk who didn't understand the concept of looking through a single lens.

To get the crowd's attention to begin their act, Rance and Abby fired their weapons heavenward while Dr. Percy cleared his throat, theatrically nodded, and began speaking slowly, distinctly, and loudly in what sounded like a mismatched mixture of a carnival barker and an erudite college professor. No matter; the people didn't care what he said, but they loved the way he said it. They were ready for a show.

As Dr. Percy was nearing the end of his teasing buildup, he gave Rance and Abby the silent signal to start walking up toward his back.

He lifted his left leg twice every so slightly, and his star performers approached the crowd.

Abby held both arms high and waved her rifle hand and her empty hand encouragingly while Rance tipped his hat and bowed every few steps. When Dr. Percy nodded to them and gracefully made his exit, his performers walked directly up to the eager onlookers.

When they were within ten feet of the first row, Rance and Abby simultaneously yelled "Now!" and spun around, swiftly pointed their weapons, and each shot three decorative cans off carts placed twenty-five feet away. Before the fans could react with applause, Rance and Abby alternately burst a row of six colorful balloons.

The crowd stood as one, applauding loudly, and shouting, "More! More!"

"Let's give 'em a show, Abby," Rance said barely above a whisper. "They'll eat it up."

The performers kept at it for another twenty minutes, shooting a variety of targets from varying distances. Then Dr. Percy reappeared, silenced everyone, and teasingly warned the onlookers the finale would be so dangerous the slightest noise from any of them could result in sudden death—*his!*

"Yes," he said in imitation of a hushed tone but loudly enough for everyone to lean forward and hear, "I have been challenged by Abby Oakley to let her shoot a cigar right out of my mouth."

Dr. Percy couldn't get another word out before a buzz of whispers built into deafening shouts of approval, mixed with more than a few pleas for them not to attempt something so dangerous. Most peeked through fingers held over their eyes, the way they would view an over-turned carriage full of passengers, or at a raging fire in a hotel full of people trapped on the top floors.

30

Dr. Percy had to fight himself to keep his feigned terrified expression from being overcome with uncontrolled laughter. He was loving every second, building up expectations as high as he dared.

Abby took Dr. Percy by the hand and appeared to drag him to the target area. She put him in position and let him go. As she turned and walked away, he ran to the crowd and wedged himself between two big men (he had hired) and looked to them for protection. Instead, they carried him bodily back to the target position, stood him in place, and dared him to move. One placed the cigar (an unusually long one) in his mouth, and Abby raised her rifle.

She aimed carefully for what seemed an eternity. Finally, she fired. But instead of a boom, all that was heard was a click. She turned to the worked-up fans, and with a shrug of her shoulders, she made a big display of taking a bullet from her belt and reloading.

Dr. Percy spat the cigar from his mouth and appeared to beg Abby to let him off. The two big men grabbed him, shoved the cigar between his clenched teeth, tied his hands behind his back, and bound his ankles so he could not run.

With showboating fanfare, Abby blasted the cigar into flying bits and pieces.

The crowd went nuts.

They loved the show.

And Dr. Percy saw the potential for his standard of living rise above the clouds.

* * *

Hours would pass before the smiles fixed on the faces of Rance, Abby, and Dr. Percy would finally relax. All three were practically giddy, but each for a different reason. Rance had conquered his nerves once he realized the patrons were with him, wanting him to be a genuine expert who would put on a big show for them. Abby relished being in the spotlight, being loved and cheered by the crowds. Dr. Percy's heart was doing a tap dance over the show getting an even better reception that he had dared dream.

All three figured things could only get better because they had not used all their showmanship yet. Rance had not performed his behind-the-back shooting tricks. Abby had not shot glass balls thrown high into the air. And Dr. Percy had not challenged onlookers to put up fifty bucks against a hundred and fifty to see if they could outshoot either Rance or Abby.

After the show and as they ate dinner in the Emerald Hotel restaurant, dozens of people lined up for autographs and to shake hands with the Traveling Sharpshooters. Abby got three requests for dates, and at least two middle-aged women kissed Dr. Percy right squarely on the mouth.

Blushing teenage girls gathered around Rance, which gave him mixed feelings. He enjoyed the attention, but he felt everyone still looked upon him as a kid. He was a man, dammit. He also noticed Abby put her arm around Dr. Percy's waist.

"I have a waist, too, you know," Rance barely kept from saying out loud.

Chapter Eight

The threat of jealousy

Rance hated to admit it, even if only to himself. But there it was, clear as spring water. He longed for more attention from Abby.

So she was five years older. So what?

So she was worlds more experienced in matters of the heart and sex. Didn't matter to him. Except that it was intimidating. He knew next-to-nothing about courting a girl, much less a woman.

And he was genuinely jealous whenever he noticed the slightest bit of affection pass between Abby and Dr. Percy, who seemed to be giving her a lot of congratulatory hugs after each of her expert and entertaining performances. Those hugs didn't appear to Rance to be exclusively congratulatory.

Abby sometimes responded with a peck of a kiss on Dr. Percy's cheek. But was it just a peck and nothing more?

Rance couldn't figure it out even though he thought about it continually. It made him moody, which both Dr. Percy and Abby noticed, and that puzzled them. They had no hint what was bothering Rance, and he was shrugging off their attempts to keep him cheerful.

All three, for their own reasons, were concerned because their performances required precision and intense concentration for Rance and Abby and peace of mind for Dr. Percy that the show leading to his dream of great riches and a high society life was not slowly coming apart.

Abby and Dr. Percy decided the time had come for them to face the problem. Truth was they were having an affair; one they were extraordinarily careful to keep Rance from finding out about. After all, it was not so much a love affair as it was a sexually gratifying outlet.

Although there was genuine affection between them, they were not in love. Furthermore, *neither wanted to be in love.* Sex had been a part of each of their lives for years. Both liked it. Missed it. Found each other sexually and intellectually stimulating and allowed themselves to get involved.

But how would they react if Rance found out? They were both intelligent and perceptive enough to guess that Rance already felt he didn't fit in. He was just an enormously talented *kid* they liked very much. And, of course, the show would fall apart without him.

"Should we just keep on and hope nothing changes?" Dr. Percy asked Abby. "Or should one or both of us have a frank talk with him and determine for sure if he is upset—or would be upset—about our being lovers?"

"Well," Abby replied, "Rance knows I have zero interest in getting married again. I've told him just enough about my former husband that he knows I am much happier single than I was married. And, no offense, Percy, but it's clear your goal is making money, not getting hitched to some female and making babies."

"Ouch!" Dr. Percy smiled. "Am I really that superficial?"

"No," Abby responded, placing her hands on his shoulders and looking straight into his beautiful pale blue eyes. "You're just honest about what you want in your life. Otherwise, I'd have no physical relationship with you at all."

"So, where does that leave us?" Dr. Percy asked. "We have to do something."

"Well, for now," Abby proposed, "let's start by treating Rance like the adult he may not yet be but wants to be considered. Make him a part of every decision about how the show is run, the towns and cities we visit, his equal share of the side money we are going to make when we start taking challenges from members of the audience.

"And I think I'll make a few suggestive advances to see if he really is interested in me and is truly jealous that you and I might be having a relationship. We may be making more of this than we need to. Rance may not care at all. He might just be homesick, lonely for people his own age, or just bored with the routine."

"All right, Abby. I trust your judgment. Just hope all of this doesn't blow up in our faces. We have a good thing going with the Traveling Sharpshooters Exhibition. We're making good money, and our prospects for performing in bigger, more lucrative arenas is becoming a reality."

Chapter Nine

Abby confronts Lance

To keep from possibly affecting Rance's performance, Abby waited until after the next show to corner him alone and confront him about his recent sulky behavior.

"All right, Rance, out with it. You've been avoiding me and Dr. Percy for a couple of weeks, hardly speaking to us, staying off by yourself, and obviously sulking about something. I have a couple of guesses, but otherwise I am at a loss to understand you.

"Talk!"

"It's nothin'," Rance said evasively. "Not worth sayin' anything about."

"The hell it's not, Rance. I think it's so potentially serious that the Traveling Sharpshooters Exhibition's future may depend on resolving whatever this is. So, please."

"If you really want to know," Rance said with no attempt to hide his anger, "the answer is you and Dr. Percy are treatin' me like a kid. You ignore me, leave me out of discussions about when and where we will appear next, and don't seem to give a hoot about what I do as long as I show up, perform well, and don't cause any trouble.

"And you two spend a lot of time together with no regard to includin' me or carin' about my life one way or another."

"How so, Rance? Be more specific. And don't hold back because you think you will hurt my feelings or make me mad at you. I assure you I will not be offended."

"Look," Rance said, while avoiding looking directly at Abby, "I know somethin' personal is goin' on between you, and I don't understand exactly why. There's five years difference between your age and mine, but Dr. Percy is at least ten years older than you.

"So why pick him and not me? You're too smart not to know I've been attracted to you since the day we first met. Dr. Percy mixes with all kinds of women in bars, at the hotels, and everywhere else he goes because he can charm all of them with his expert use of the language and his experience in dealin' with people of all education and financial levels.

"I have nobody. He's just usin' you, and I would not do that. So why him and not me?"

Not anticipating Rance would be so direct, Abby takes a moment to form a reply. It has to be said just right. She can't patronize him. He would catch on in an instant and perhaps bitterly demand why she confronted him if she didn't want to hear the truth.

"Rance, I am going to give you a complete and honest answer. It will take me a few minutes because I have not thought it through. I do not know how much you want to hear, but I'll presume it's everything. So, listen without interrupting me or getting mad at me or having your feelings hurt. I promise I will sit right here and listen to everything you say when I'm finished. All right?"

"All right," Rance replied eagerly, even though he was anxious, too, because he felt so inferior to Abby in life experiences.

"Rance, even though I am only five years your senior, there is a world of difference between us in our experiences with romance and sex. I was married when I was seventeen. I was very much in love with a man who was a widower even though he was only twenty-five, and he taught me beginning on our wedding night what intimate relations beween a man and a woman were all about.

"I started out knowing nothing. The same point I am all but certain you are now. I know you've never had a steady girlfriend, and until now you have lived at home all your life under the supervision of your parents. By the time I was nineteen, as you are now, I had had sex hundreds of times.

"You still have not had that even once, unless you have sneaked into a brothel a time or two during our travels. I'm certain you have not done that yet, and I hope you won't. There's no love there, only the real danger of disease. Those women don't give a hoot about the men they're with. They just want to get things over as soon as possible, collect their money, and move on quickly to the next guy."

Rance's mind wandered momentarily to an experience he had had a few weeks prior, but he wasn't about to share it with Abby. She was correct when she presumed he had not turned to prostitutes for sex. He was afraid of disease, and he wanted romantic sex, not a quick rutting.

What he did not reveal to Abby was that he had paid a lady of the evening one time, but when he got into a room alone with her and she started her routine with him, he stretched out his arms with the palms of his hands turned upward to tell her without words to keep her distance.

"I'm payin' for advice only," he informed her.

Looking surprised and more than a little suspicious, she said almost in a challenge: "Like what?"

"Nothin' weird," he assured her. "I want to find out somethin' that you know from your experience. I have no one in my family or in my circle of friends I can ask. And I don't want to go to a library to see if I can find a book to tell me what I want to know."

"Well, what is it?" she asked. "You're paying for it, so I'll tell you if I know."

Blushing with embarrassment and feeling some humiliation, Rance got it out.

"Well, you can see that I am a small man. I haven't had sex yet, and what I want to know is if a man's height has anything to do with how big his, uh, sex organ is? Will women bigger than me laugh at my size? I've been worryin' about that for years because I don't know how big is normal."

The woman, who went by the name of Mary and appeared to be in her late 20s or early thirties, grasped the sincerity of his question, and answered honestly. "No, how tall a man is does not necessarily relate to the size of his, as you put it, sex organ. They come in different sizes, and how a man performs sex is more important than how big he is.

"How big are you?" she wanted to know.

Rance turned crimson.

"You're never going to see me again, so let's have a look. Or if you are too embarrassed, I can tell by a feel," she said while undressing to make sure he would get into an excited state. Then with practiced hands, she felt thoroughly through his clothing and smiled.

"You've got plenty. Don't ever worry about that again."

"Rance!" Abby shouted. "Aren't you listening to me? I'm trying to tell you something I think you need to know."

"Sorry, Abby," Rance apologized. "I didn't know if you were tryin' to get me to confirm I had not been to a pleasure house, and I was trying to think of a polite way of sayin' why I have not. The words I was searchin' for were 'romantic sex' because that's the only kind I want. I didn't want to use the dirty words they use in those places.

"And I guess I was tryin' to keep you from telling me what I think I've already guessed."

"Well, I'm going to tell you anyway, Rance. Our futures—yours, mine, and Dr. Percy's—might depend on how you take this. You see, that five years difference in our ages is only chronological; we're light years apart in experience. To be frank to the point of shocking you, the simple truth is, I am having sex with Dr. Percy simply because I like it, I like him and find him attractive, but we are not in love and never will be.

"He wants to make a fortune. Period. He has zero interest in falling in love and especially getting married and being bogged down financially by a woman and inevitably children. I feel exactly the same way, only I never want to be married again. I never want to be dependent ever again on any man for my livelihood. I am my own boss now, and I damned sure plan to stay that way.

"I'm young and Dr. Percy is not yet middle aged. I am determined to stay single, and so is he—or at least until he has reached a point of absolute financial security.

'You, Rance, on the other hand, are infatuated with me. I saw it the first day we met. But because of your age and your inexperience, you could easily confuse infatuation with love. That would lead to jealousy—the kind I think you already have about me and Dr. Percy. And that would destroy our show just when it is becoming so popular and making good money for all of us.

"I have not been consciously treating you 'like a kid.' Only as an inexperienced young man. You are good-looking, unbelievably kind and considerate—even protective of me. I like being around you. And it goes without saying, you are the most talented man with a pistol I've ever seen.

"Finally, Rance, please know that although I had sex hundreds of times when I was married, I was faithful to my husband. I have never been promiscuous. I was a virgin on my wedding night, and I have had sex with only two men since my divorce. But as I said, even though I do not intend to ever get married again, I like romantic sex and I'm not going to live without it.

"So now it's your turn, Rance. After hearing all this, what do you expect of me? What do you want of me?"

"Abby," Rance started, still avoiding eye contact and unable to fully keep from trembling noticeably, "I want what I suppose you are tellin' me I can't have. I want you, I think about you all the time, imaginin' what it would be like to hold you, hug you and kiss you. And someday gettin' to touch you intimately and make love to you. Sometimes, it drives me crazy.

"Travelin' all the time, I have no chance to meet young women, or women of any age or kind. And you are right that I have never had sex, and that I would never go to a brothel. I consider that repulsive.

"I'm lonely. I'm homesick. I have nothin' to do but practice, perform, and travel. Then practice, perform, and travel some more. As you know, I do go to church whenever we have a Sunday mornin' free, and I have checked to see if a church is havin' a potluck luncheon where I can meet young women. But their fathers and their older brothers always make it clear that I am welcome to eat with them, but their daughters and sisters are off limits to a travelin' trick shot artist.

"For years, I couldn't wait to join a group like ours and travel all over gettin' applause and praise for my skills. But I never considered for a moment what the rest of my life would be like. I have to say, I don't like it.

"You have your personal, professional, and intimate relationship with Dr. Percy, and that seems to be fulfillin' all your needs. That's your business. The fact that I am envious doesn't give me the right to sulk around and cause tension.

"I guess I'd best go home and try livin' like my mom and dad and my brother Tyrone do. He's plannin' to get married soon, and my parents have already given permission to Taylor to marry when she turns sixteen soon."

"Please, Rance. Please wait until I have had a chance to talk with Dr. Percy. I can't carry this show alone, and he still hasn't found any others to join us. Give us some time. Promise?"

"Of course I will, Abby. I need time myself to do some more thinkin' of my own."

Chapter Ten

Sharpshooters add a member who doesn't shoot

Dr. Percy's long search for a third team member finally materialized, but with a couple of almost astonishing twists—neither of which involved a sharpshooter.

One Saturday evening after Rance and Abby had dazzled an appreciative audience in El Paso, Dr. Percy was approached in his hotel lobby by an impressive looking, richly dressed Mexican who appeared to be in his mid-forties. He also appeared to be well educated because he exhibited a precise knowledge of English grammar and pronunciation.

"Senor Hardcastle, may I have a moment of your time, if you please?"

"Certainly, sir," Dr. Percy replied, a little taken aback that for the first time in a long while since he came West, someone addressed him by his last name. "What may I do for you?"

"My name is Lorenzo Antonio Guerrero, and I hope, senor, it is I who can do something for you. I have heard you have put out word you are seeking to expand your Traveling Sharpshooters Exhibition. Is that so, sir?"

"It is, and please call me Dr. Percy as everyone else does."

"Thank you, sir, and my friends call me Lorenzo."

"Well, Lorenzo, tell me what proficiency you have with weapons?"

"Very little, Dr. Percy. But I have a skill I think you and your audiences would find very entertaining if you will give me an opportunity to demonstrate it. But may I keep it a secret until you have seen it because I am afraid you would turn me down without otherwise giving me a chance."

"Well, Lorenzo, I am doing nothing until I have dinner at about eight o'clock, so where do we go for the demonstration?"

"It is but a short distance, Dr. Percy. If you will please walk with me."

Making small talk as they walked, Lorenzo leads Dr. Percy through the middle of town and turns left, going about a quarter of a mile to an open grassy area with stables and a large corral where Lorenzo places two fingers into his mouth and gives three brief, sharp whistles. Dr. Percy is intrigued, not quite expecting what he'll see but presuming it will be an animal of some sort.

His presumption is correct, but no guess on his part would have prepared him for the spirited, prancing appearance of a fine horse obviously of superior bearing. It is an Andalusian breed, known for its intelligence, strong build, and docile behavior. It stands fifteen and a half hands (about six feet) and weighs approximately eleven hundred pounds. It is gray with a thick mane and tail. His name is Amado, which means beloved.

Amado trots over to Lorenzo, whinnies, and stomps his right front hoof twice. That's his signal for two lumps of the sugar his owner habitually carries in one of his pockets. Lorenzo happily complies. Amado makes short work of those two lumps and stomps his hoof twice again. "No, no, my friend," Lorenzo says with a laugh. "First, you have to remember your manners.

"Please greet our new friend, Dr. Percy."

Amado responds with a bow that lasts three seconds and stomps his hoof twice again.

"I told you before, no, no, no," Lorenzo says while turning his back and walking away from the beautiful horse. Amado follows, inserts his head between Lorenzo's legs and tosses him gently into the air.

Lorenzo walks faster. So does Amado and performs the same stunt two more times. The performance earns him two additional lumps of sugar.

"Now, Amado, dance for Dr. Percy. Up! Up!" Amado responds by rearing on his back legs and taking several steps forward. "Now, dressage, Amado." The horse again transfers his weight to his hindquarters, lifts vertically and kicks out, a very impressive and difficult move.

After another reward, this time a small carrot, Amado performs a series of playful tricks his owner assures Dr. Percy audiences will love. Amado can "play dead" like a dog, roll onto his back and whinny loudly while flailing his legs around, and with Lorenzo sitting on him backward and steering with the horse's tail, Amado moves left, right, forward, and backward following the tugs being made by Lorenzo.

Dr. Percy has seen enough. He invites Lorenzo to have dinner with him and to talk over business.

* * *

While eating fine food and enjoying a vintage wine, Dr. Percy and Lorenzo get to know each other. Dr. Percy provides his essential background information and his goals, leaving out nothing important, including his desire to earn a fortune and live well for the rest of his life.

"I appreciate your frankness and your honesty, my new friend," Lorenzo says. "My life is easy to explain. You asked how I came to speak English so well. It is because I am the son of a diplomat. My father has served as a representative of our government in Washington, D.C., for more than thirty years. I went to private schools there and received the same education as the privileged children of the politically powerful and the wealthy businessmen. I have spent three-quarters of my life in the United States, serving mostly as my father's executive assistant.

"My family is, as you say in this country, well to do. I am married to my wife, Alexia, and we have one seventeen-year-old daughter, Antonella, which means daughter of Antonio. And it is for her benefit that I seek to join your Exhibition for a brief period of perhaps a year. Salary is no issue. I will accept whatever you can afford to pay."

Antonella, Lorenzo explains, has gotten a taste for the life of show business from the free performances she and Lorenzo have given with Amado for children in schools and in hospitals, and at church functions both in the United States and in Mexico.

"It is her wish for her eighteenth birthday several months from now."

"I will have an answer for you tomorrow, Lorenzo," Dr. Percy promises, "after I have had a discussion with Abby and Rance."

"By the way," Lorenzo mentions in passing, with a quizzical look of amusement, "I have the name of a man of unusual talents you may be interested in adding to your group, if you have room for him. But that's a topic for another day, if you care to hear about him."

Chapter Eleven

The Guerreros and their stunning daughter

Both Rance and Abby were genuinely surprised at Dr. Percy's suggestion that they add Senor Lorenzo Antonio Guerrero and his magnificent horse to their group.

"I took it for granted you were looking for an expert shooter from a different ethnic background," Abby said. "But I must say I love having more of a novelty act. Everybody in the West is accustomed to being around horses, and I think adults and children alike will find Amado entertaining."

Rance agreed, adding with a slightly guilty admission that he was glad Dr. Percy did not choose another sharpshooter audiences would inevitably compare with him and Abby.

"You feel the same way, Abby?" Dr. Percy inquired.

"Absolutely. And the fact that he isn't asking for a big slice of our pie is a positive factor, too," she admitted. "Rubbing shoulders with members of a prominent Mexican family will also be a good experience for us as well as for our audiences.

"When are you going to tell him?"

"At lunch today, and I want both of you to be with me. That would make a nice welcome for him and his family. His wife, Alexia, and his daughter, Antonella, will be there, too."

"How old is Lorenzo's daughter, and what does she look like?" Rance inquired with an expression that shamelessly exposed his motives.

"Seventeen. Almost eighteen, I think Lorenzo said. Lorenzo is a good-looking gentleman in his forties, but I have not met Alexia or

Antonella. So, what they look like will be as much of a surprise to me as to you."

* * *

Senora Guerrero was a small woman with a trim figure, dark eyes, and shoulder length, wavy brown hair streaked with gray. She was quite pretty, had a warm smile so wide it exposed almost all of her teeth, and she carried herself with enormous self assurance and pride. Her very presence commanded respect, but it was a deference she had experienced all of her life, so she was not haughty but surprisingly relaxed and friendly.

Rance turned beet red when Antonella looked straight at him while giving only a nod and a smile to Dr. Percy and Abby. She expected the expert shooter to be much older than she was and was happy to learn he was someone near her age. "And he's cute, too," she silently concluded.

A stuttering "puh-pleased to meet you" was the best Rance could manage, and he was already mentally kicking himself for coming off as such an awkward dunce. He almost wished she were ugly, so he could be indifferent and therefore unaffected.

None of this interaction escaped the attention of the four older adults, and their smiles revealed their amusement. Abby was not only amused but also got a rush of relief. If Rance kept his attention focused on Antonella, it wouldn't be on her.

The reason for Rance's reticence was evident. Antonella was stunning!

She was able to maintain her composure better than Rance because she had always been stunning and had long been accustomed to the stares she attracted. But she had been reared by expert female relatives and governesses to act like a lady of culture and superior bearing that promoted confidence restricted respectfully by a degree of humility.

Like her mother, Antonella was short. A quality Lance not only admired but was grateful for, given his modest height. She also had wavy brown hair and dark sparkling eyes. Unlike her mother, however, Antonella was blessed more generously by Nature with considerably more roundness in the chest and hips, adding to her desirability. All the Guerreros had skin the tan color white people hoped to turn in the summertime. And their dress was impeccably stylish and expensive. They looked like aristocrats.

Audiences will be very impressed with the Guerreros, Dr. Percy, Abby, and Rance all concluded without having to say so.

Lunch passed pleasantly. Dr. Percy announced with his usual flair that the Traveling Sharpshooters Exhibition would be honored to add the Guerreros to its roster. They smiled their acceptance, and Lorenzo added a simple "Gracias."

Seated beside Rance, Antonella initiated a conversation by inquiring about Rance's shooting skills, how he acquired them, and how he applied them in his act. She was gifted at conversation and had learned from her female elders that even shy men enjoy talking about their work and accomplishments.

"I can't wait to see you perform," she told him excitedly. "I've never before met anyone with your skills," she explained.

Rance invited her to watch him at their practice session later on in the afternoon and asked if her father would be putting Amado through his routine then, too.

"Partly," she answered with a sly smile.

"I don't understand," Rance responded.

"Father works with Amado for part of the act, and I do another part. It was my idea, Rance, for father to ask to join your troupe because I love show business. I asked for my eighteenth birthday that we take a year performing full time with Amado instead of just putting on an occasional show as we've been doing, mostly for school children. Amado is so beautiful and amazing, everyone from the smallest child to the oldest adult falls in love with him.

"So, yes, we will be at the practice this afternoon. I look forward to seeing you there."

"Me, too," Rance said, perhaps with a tad too much enthusiasm. He had already concluded that God could not have formed any other young woman more suited for him in beauty, size, and in the way she comported herself.

Once again, however, Rance was acutely aware that just as he was separated by age and experience from Abby, he had obvious challenges if he were to pursue Antonella. She was from a wealthy, aristocratic, socially, and politically prominent family and was far more refined and educated than he was.

Actually, Rance had even bigger obstacles than his background as an unsophisticated rural American. He was completely unaware that families like the Guerreros did not permit their daughters to go anywhere with a man without being properly chaperoned. Eyes would be upon both young people anytime and all of the time they were together.

Chapter Twelve

A double success could become a triple

Dr. Percy considered his latest acquisition of talent to be a double success—one that he intentionally sought, and the other a welcome surprise. Because the Guerreros are Mexican, his group added an ethnicity that made them different from similar groups of professional shooters. That the talent was an animal act made his team not only more appealing to audiences but also to the businessmen who sponsored these exhibitions.

If he could offer a fourth different act with yet another ethnicity, Dr. Percy could present a unique troupe of performers that should be even more in demand. Furthermore, with four performers, he would have enough depth of talent to expand to two performances a day at each exhibition, thereby doubling his number of paying customers, many of whom would attend both shows for a special rate because the second act would not just be a duplicate of the first.

Understandably, Dr. Percy was eager to learn something about the performer Lorenzo said he might be interested in because the man had unusual skills.

"Because you have told me of your desire to have an eclectic mix of performers, I am happy to inform you that the man I speak of is a Navajo Indian," Lorenzo said expectantly.

"Wow!" was the only word that an excited Dr. Percy could draw from his vast knowledge of the English language. "What can he do, Lorenzo? I can't wait to hear."

"He is an expert with a lance and a tomahawk."

"How does he use them? I presume he throws them at targets."

Lorenzo bursts into laughter. "Prepare yourself, my friend. He has a big circular wooden bullseye target that he puts his wife in front of and throws tomahawks and lances as close to her as he dares without maiming or killing her. It's very dangerous and therefore very suspenseful and exciting. Audiences literally hold their breath during most of the performance."

"Who is this man, where does he live, and how soon can we contact him, Lorenzo?"

"His name is Ahiga and he lives with his wife, Dezba, in northern Arizona. You will like both names. His means 'he fights' and hers means 'going to war.' I know how to get in touch with him."

"Well, please do so without delay. With him added to you and Antonella, Rance, and Abby, we will have the best show in the entire West. If we can get enough attention, I am confident we could be the primary act in the biggest shows in this part of the country. Maybe in the East as well."

Lorenzo slapped Dr. Percy on the back, gave him a hand-on-the-shoulder hug and said, "You dream big, my friend. I like that. Yes, I do indeed."

* * *

More than a month had passed since Lorenzo sent his letter to his Indian friend, but he had gotten no response from Ahiga. However, that space of time was not so unusual given the unreliability of the mail system. But, as a precaution against the letter being lost or Ahiga and Dezba being away performing at some shows, Lorenzo wrote again.

"Do not worry just yet, amigo," Lorenzo reassured Dr. Percy. "I will continue to contact Ahiga, and he is most dependable. He will get back to us regardless of whether he is interested in the possibility of joining us. Anyway, we are doing quite well since Antonella and I joined you and Rance and Abby, no?"

"Better than just well, Lorenzo. Our bookings are improving in both quantity and quality. More important," Dr. Percy grinned, "at least as far as my avaricious heart is concerned, we're bringing in much more money. But I still don't feel comfortable trying to expand to two shows a day without another act. Hope your friend and his wife are available soon."

Lorenzo's assessment about the expanded acts' growing popularity and success was an understatement. Rance and Abby were as popular as ever, despite the fact that he was still withholding for just the right time his behind-the-back shots and Abby had not yet shot glass balls out of the air. They planned with Dr. Percy to save those for two-a-day performances.

Audiences everywhere were immediately receptive to the intelligent and humorous act Lorenzo and Antonella displayed with the magnificent Amado. As expected, people of all ages were delighted. When Amado stomped his hoof to ask for a treat, children identified with him because they often had to beg for sweets, too. All the other tricks Lorenzo had demonstrated when he first auditioned for Dr. Percy appealed to the audiences as well.

When Antonella took her turn working with Amado, she looked so small beside the big horse, the onlookers wondered how she would be able to handle him. With love was the answer. It became evident immediately that the pretty little human and the horse eleven times her weight had an affectionate relationship.

Dr. Percy had a role in this part of the act, too. Speaking loudly, he repeated Antonella's commands to Amado, first when she told Amado to sit on his hindquarters like a dog. On her signal, he trotted over to face Antonella and shook his head no. No, he would not do it. She asked him again, and again he shook his head vigorously from side to side, unmistakably refusing to cooperate.

Pretending to be frustrated, Antonella turned to the audience and shrugged, as if she were giving up. "What will it take," she asked the animal, "for you to do as I ask?"

Without hesitation, Amado stomped his right front hoof twice. Antonella threw her arms upward in defeat, reached into her pocket and produced two sugar cubes. She stretched out her hand to Amado and asked: "Now will you sit?" He gobbled down the sugar, shook his head up and down several times and obediently sat on his rear.

The crowd loved it, especially when she unsuccessfully instructed him repeatedly to stand. He shook his head no and refused to budge. "What if I give you a carrot?" Antonella offered. Amado enthusiastically shook his head yes, chewed the carrot noisily and jumped back onto all four hoofs.

No face in the crowd looked happier and more thrilled than Rance's. He was smiling from ear to ear, clapping his hands, and shouting approvingly.

The look on Rance's face pleased no one more than it did Abby. Rance obviously had another romantic interest, praise the Lord. Since Antonella joined the team, it was clear to Abby that Rance was treating her more like a respected colleague than a potential lover.

As closely as her parents guarded her and her reputation by constantly keeping her in their sight, Antonella, Abby had happily observed, still managed to hold Rance's hand beneath the dinner table.

It was a near perfect evening for the Traveling Sharpshooters Exhibition as they made their next performance in the notorious town of Deadwood, South Dakota, where the folk hero Wild Bill Hickok was murdered in 1876.

Near perfect, that is, until it ended in death.

Chapter Thirteen

A dangerous challenge

After a dozen or so exhibitions in which Rance and Abby performed almost flawlessly, Dr. Percy figured his two sharpshooters were comfortable enough before audiences to take on challengers willing to put up fifty dollars each. Few were willing to risk the equivalent of a cowboy's monthly pay against the chance of winning one hundred fifty dollars. But in the bigger cities, a couple of the locals handy with a pistol or a rifle always stepped up. And lost.

Things went well for several months. It was in Deadwood at the end of the regular performances that Rance met an unexpected and dangerous challenge. A professional gambler known for picking fights with and killing opponents who won too much of his money pushed ahead of two other challengers and ceremoniously dared Dr. Percy to put up two thousand dollars against his seven hundred.

Dr. Percy managed to keep a straight face but gulped almost loudly enough to be heard. Tams Coaltrane, better known as "Nitro" because of his explosive temper, waved seven one-hundred-dollar bills at the crowd and then within a foot of Dr. Percy's nose.

That got the attention of Sheriff Ashton Hardy and his deputy, Jaxon Lewis. They knew beyond doubt that Nitro would not bow out gracefully if he lost to Rance. So as discreetly as possible with hundreds of people watching, the lawmen walked slowly up to Nitro, and the sheriff said barely above a whisper: "Nitro, be advised that me and Jaxon here are gonna have our eyes on you and our guns at the ready if you cause any trouble of any kind." Nitro's response was a disrespectful sneer.

Dr. Percy took Rance aside, explained who his opponent was, and offered to turn down the challenge. "No, sir," Rance said. "If we do that, word will get around, and that would pretty much put us out of the challenge business."

With some trepidation that he kept to himself, Dr. Percy waved his arms to get everyone's attention, flashed what he hoped would be a confident smile, and explained how the match would work. With what the onlookers considered a fortune at stake, they quieted and with un-divided attention listened to the instructions.

"In Stage One, each contestant will draw on my count of three and shoot six bottles off his cart, set the same distance away as the other cart. Then, if need be, we will move the carts ten feet farther away and have the same kind of targets. If necessary, we will have a third match and move the targets back another ten feet.

"If at any point, either man misses a target or misses more than his opponent, the match is over.

"Gentlemen, take your positions fifteen feet apart behind the line you see in front of you. Fire on my count of three."

To create as much tension among the onlookers as possible, Dr. Percy cautioned them to "hold your breath and make no noise whatso-ever as I command the countdown."

Heavy breathing and the chirping of a few birds were the only sounds the shooters could hear.

"One, two, THREE!" Dr. Percy yelled. Two blazing fast draws and twelve exploding jars ended with shattered glass all over the carts. A tie.

Rance and Nitro reloaded and prepared to step up the challenge at more distant targets. Another tie.

Waiting until the crowd settled down while milking every drop of drama he could squeeze, Dr. Percy gave the countdown again. This time, Rance clearly outdrew Nitro and finished first. To remove all doubt, Rance hit all six targets, and Nitro missed one.

Dr. Percy held up Rance's shooting arm and paraded him around to the deafening cheers of the crowd. But when Rance walked over to show good sportsmanship by shaking hands with Nitro, he was met with a totally unexpected challenge—unexpected that is by everyone but the sheriff and his deputy. They moved into a position that gave them an unobstructed view of Nitro.

Nitro waved his arms at the crowd, quieted them, and then said as loud as his lungs allowed: "This kid is good with a gun. I'll give him that. But the real test of a man and his gun is when he faces another man and his gun with each one's life on the line.

"So, sharpshooter, let's see who's the better man in a real gunfight. That is if you aren't too chicken-shit to face me."

Rance did not know what to say. He never expected this. He was taken completely by surprise and certainly did not want to either kill a man or be killed himself. It was against his principles. He shot targets, not a human being he'd known for only a half hour.

"I'm not going to fight you to the death, mister," Rance said without shame. "We have no reason to do this. It was just a shooting match."

Squaring himself off about twenty feet from Rance and motioning everyone else out of the way, Nitro warned: "We've both reloaded, so it will be a fair fight. Either draw or die, boy. I'm going for my gun."

Before Nitro could complete his draw, two shots rang out simultaneously, and both hit the gambler in the chest, knocking him to the ground with fatal wounds. Those bullets, however, did not come from Rance, but from the two lawmen. They anticipated Nitro's reaction to losing and were prepared for it.

Even though they had no part in the killing, Abby, Dr. Percy, and the Guererros left Deadwood in a state of shock. Rance left fundamentally changed.

From his earliest days of exhibition shooting competition, he became aware that a few of his opponents were killers eagerly building their reputations as gunfighters. Showing off their skills in exhibitions was one way of getting noticed. He feared that if he made them look bad, they might force him into a deadly gunfight.

Were it not for the sheriff and his deputy, that deadly fight would have come on this day. Rance, Abby, and Dr. Percy would have to be constantly on guard and perhaps hire local off-duty lawmen to be on standby during future performances and challenges.

Rance also decided to downplay his growing reputation by dressing in ordinary farmer's clothing while not performing so he would not be easily recognized and thereby not so tempting a challenge for the reputation-seekers.

The "disguise" worked effectively—until he found himself in the wrong bar at the wrong time, facing that giant bully in Santa Fe.

Chapter Fourteen

Rance at a crossroads

Rance's life was at a crossroads. Despite the presence of beautiful and friendly Antonella, he remained lonely and homesick. He had not seen his family in nearly two years. He had little hope of anything serious or long-term developing between him and Antonella. They had to sneak to hold hands under the dinner table and had not come close to having their first kiss, even though he was certain she was as willing as he was.

Her mother watched her like a hawk, and her dad had declared that after their year with the Traveling Sharpshooters Exhibition, he was going to leave his job in Washington and return to Mexico to take charge of his family's ranches and other holdings. Lorenzo's only brother was in failing health and their father would not leave the diplomatic service as long as he was still needed.

In addition, Antonella's mother had made clear she was determined for her daughter to marry soon to a man of her own class and social and economic standing. Rance's qualifications did not match a single one of Alexia's standards.

Rance's love of performing had not changed, and he remained the key member of the Traveling Sharpshooters Exhibition. But now he faced the constant danger of being goaded into deadly gunfights. Before the episode with Nitro, that fear was hypothetical. Now it was real.

Should he resign, put his guns aside, and catch the next train home? Settle for the ordinary life of a gunsmith like his dad and brother? Perhaps become a storekeeper, or operate a livery stable? Get married and have kids? Become a deacon in the church and live a simple life?

If he made that radical change, he could start with a big nest egg he had saved up so far, but he never would make much more money than it took to raise a family and look forward to a modest retirement. He would not have the fame he had gained on the exhibition shooting circuit. Being praised. Honored. Respected. Perhaps even a little bit feared.

He would be giving up any chance of gaining Abby's affection and love—not that she had so far given any indication he stood a chance. And despite what he knew was Antonella's sincere romantic interest in him, she was a member of a class in which the young women were not in charge of their future. If she ran away with Rance, her family would disown her. She loved them too much to risk that.

And what about Dr. Percy and his dreams of great riches and the high life? He had been good to both Rance and Abby. Fair and aboveboard in all of their dealings, always keeping his word. Would it be honorable to just walk off and leave both Dr. Percy and Abby on their own?

Without Rance, the show would not be attractive enough to bring in the big dollars, including the increasing income Rance was making from challenges. He already had several thousand dollars in savings and could make a great deal more as their team's growing reputation was gaining them invitations to bigger events and even calls for more private exhibitions for cattle and oil rich families who could afford to hire them for their get-togethers.

In addition, one of the wealthy oilmen Dr. Percy had gotten to know well had offered him a chance to invest ten thousand dollars in an oil well venture. Dr. Percy in turn offered Rance and Abby a chance to put in two thousand, five hundred dollars each. Both decided to take the gamble.

Rance concluded he wasn't yet ready to make a decision about leaving the show. "I'll finish out the season and give myself time to know for sure what I want to do, as well as give Dr. Percy and Abby plenty of time to make other arrangements for the team if I do leave."

Perhaps if the addition of Ahiga and Dezba came about, it would be enough to enable Dr. Percy and Abby to continue the show successfully. But could they find another horse act to replace Amado, Lorenzo, and Antonella?

"All of this speculation is just making me feel more anxious," Rance concluded. "Best I just hang around awhile and see what happens. But the first thing I'm gonna do at the end of the exhibition season is go home. At least it feels good to know I don't have to come back to the show if that's not what I want."

Chapter Fifteen

Ahiga and Dezba join the team

A month-old letter from Ahiga finally catches up with Lorenzo when the team is performing in San Antonio while touring the Southwest during the colder late Fall months. It is brief and positive: "My wife and I can meet you in San Antonio during your scheduled period of October 25-28. Please inform Dr. Percy we will come prepared to audition, and if we are acceptable to him and the financial arrangements are satisfactory, we would be happy, old friend, to join you and your family and the others as part of the Traveling Sharpshooters Exhibition."

Lorenzo, Alexia, and Antonella were pleased. Dr. Percy was elated. And Rance and Abby saw this expansion as a lucky break leading to two performances a day and a significantly greater income.

When the Navajos arrived, they were welcomed like dear old friends by the Guerreros, and Ahiga surprised everybody by looking scarier than hell in his tribal dress. Dr. Percy was overjoyed because he believed that scary effect would translate tenfold on the audiences. He realized customers love to be frightened when they know they are really safe in their seats.

Rance and Abby weren't so sure.

"They may scare the children so much, their parents won't bring them or themselves to the show, Rance," Abby worried. Rance expressed the same misgivings.

In reality, Ahiga and Dezba were as normal and as civilized as the rest of the group. Both had been performing around mostly white audiences for a long time. Both spoke English quite well except their vocabularies were limited and their pronunciations were not perfect.

But Dr. Percy concluded their personal appearance would be no problem. He did virtually all of the publicity and public speaking for his team, and he was a master at it. In addition, he saw a way to tone down the crowd's reactions without totally giving up the potential scariness he wanted customers to feel.

"Debza, I want to outfit you in a costume suitable for an Indian princess. Beautiful tan leather with intricate beading, matching moccasins, a headband with one simple Eagle feather, turquoise bracelets and necklaces, a touch of eye and lip makeup, and long braided hair. You will not be scary in the least. Everyone will see you as the gorgeous, sympathetic target of your husband and his tomahawks and lances.

"Ahiga, I'd like to experiment with your threatening look for the first performance and see how it goes over. I want you in traditional Navajo war paint, shirtless with a breastplate, and whatever headdress you think is appropriate. By the way, Ahiga, what are those breastplates made of?"

"Many things, Dr. Percy. Animal bones, shells, beads, and other objects held together by leather. The people we've performed before are fascinated by them."

"All right then, let's all gather at the showgrounds after lunch and watch Ahiga and Dezba give us a performance. Then we will give them an abbreviated look at what we do.

"I don't know about all of you, but I suspect you are as excited as I am about our prospects for becoming the leading traveling exhibition in the West. And soon."

* * *

After carefully watching Ahiga and Debza perform, Dr. Percy decided to place them last among the four performances for two reasons: For one, their act is so extraordinarily exciting. For the other, it is so authentically dangerous he doesn't want to risk a serious accident from ruining or even canceling the rest of the performances.

Rance, who will open the show, and Abby, who will go second and precede Lorenzo and Antonella's horse act, fully agree with Dr. Percy's lineup. Both had not only held their breath during Ahiga and Debza's practice performances but also were tempted to look away after they saw how narrowly Ahiga was missing Debza's body and limbs.

Abby only half jokingly whispered in an aside to Rance and Dr. Percy that if she were Debza, she'd be "damned careful about making him angry at her right before a show."

The arena in San Antonio was large enough to accommodate a huge crowd, bringing in record gate receipts, plus whatever individuals purchased among the numerous items Dr. Percy was selling on the side. To continue to attract such a throng, Dr. Percy's offering for the first time of four distinct acts had better live up to all the hype he had poured into it.

Rance, in all of his flashy finery, performed perfectly without missing a shot at both stationary and moving targets. His fast draw wowed the young and had old-timers comparing him to the fastest they'd ever seen anywhere. And because the troupe had so much riding on this uniquely important performance, he displayed for the first time his behind-the-back trick shot.

Onlookers screamed their heads off and pounded their hands together until they hurt. The only downside was that two of the four men who had put up fifty dollars each to challenge Rance asked to withdraw and get their money back. The other two, as expected, lost to Rance very quickly.

Appearing in her sparkly outfit that she loved even though she still called it gaudy, Abby took the stage with her rifle that looked to the crowd to be about as long as she was tall. If anyone in the audience had passed her on the street without knowing who she was, they would have perhaps noticed only that she was a pretty little woman. No one would guess she would be a star attraction of the Traveling Sharpshooters Exhibition.

But when she turned that rifle every which way but loose, they became believers as she hit target after target without a miss. And as was the case at all previous shows around the West, her crowd's favorite trick was her shooting a cigar out of Dr. Percy's clinched teeth with him following his routine of being scared to the point of fleeing until a couple of tough men tied him in place.

Abby still withheld shooting glass objects tossed into the air. She was saving it for the second act when the group started doing two-a-day performances.

The crowd stared in confusion when Lorenzo and Antonella followed Abby. They were impressed with the big, beautiful horse, but they looked in vain for pistols and rifles. The man and the young woman had not a single one on their persons or on the horse.

But as Lorenzo had promised at his first meeting with Dr. Percy, the onlookers of all ages soon fell in love with the playful Amado. He had them oohing and aahing when he accomplished his difficult jumps and kicks, and they laughed with glee when he shook his head "yes" or "no" and stomped his right front hoof twice, refusing to do anything without a reward of the treats of sugar lumps and carrots.

This part of the show provided a delightful pause between the gun-smoke acts and the last to follow—one that Dr. Percy had promised loudly and frequently all over town the previous four days would be the most dangerous any audience members had ever witnessed.

When workers unveiled the huge circular wooden target wheel with bullseye circles, drummers placed throughout the arena started pounding tom-toms with a ferocious, deafening beat intended to get hearts ticking fast and at least tinges of fear invading every body in the seats. Some men put their arms around the wives, and parents held their children close.

Looking beautiful in her princess outfit and carefully applied makeup that accentuated her exotic look, Debza walked slowly over to the target and placed herself in front of it. People caught on immediately, and shock registered throughout the area. *She was the target!* Her husband was going to throw tomahawks and lances in her direction, risking maiming or killing her.

The drumbeat rolled thunderously again as the muscular Ahiga ran rapidly on stage carrying a lance in one hand and a tomahawk in the other. He was big, carried battle scars on his face and arms and looked threatening in his war paint and warrior's outfit. The expression on his face as he turned slowly on all sides gave the spectators the cruelest, most barbaric glare most of them had ever imagined.

Wasting no time to apparently aim, Ahiga threw a tomahawk that stuck between Debza's right arm and her body. Quickly again, he tossed another in the same place between her other arm and body. Onlookers shrieked in unison—just as Ahiga knew they would, and Dr. Percy hoped they would.

After sticking other tomahawks beside each hip, Ahiga spun totally around and unleashed a fifth tomahawk between her feet, drawing a small amount of "blood" from an oversized moccasin filled with red liquid. More than one onlooker fainted.

Ahiga turned to the crowd and grunted seemingly angrily at them, like a dog barking, when large numbers of them began accusing him of trying to kill his wife.

He responded by tossing to the ground his remaining two tomahawks, walking over to a nearby table and picking up four lances, shaking them at the crowd. Their reaction had the hearts of Rance, Abby, Lorenzo, Alexia, and Antonella pounding as one with the crowd's.

With practiced fanfare, acting as if lance throwing for him was much harder than it actually was, Ahiga slowly took aim, and ran five paces toward Debza and rocketed a spear within four inches of the top of her head. She did not flinch.

He ran five more paces sideways to his right and landed a lance between her knees.

For his final throws, Ahiga ran to the edge of the arena. Some thought he was trying to get away before the crowd wanted him to leave. Instead, he mounted a horse bareback while holding a lance in each hand, guided the horse with his knees until it was heading straight toward his wife while he let out a blood-curdling war cry. When he was about fifteen feet away, he threw both lances simultaneously, landing each less than a shoulder's width beside Debza's neck.

As the spectators allowed themselves to breathe again, they jumped to their feet and applauded wildly as Ahiga slid off his horse, gathered Debza in his arms, swirled her around in an embrace, and walked over to the crowd taking bows with his wife to the whistles, yells, and booming clapping of the appreciative crowd.

Other members of his troupe were euphoric with happiness. As for Dr. Percy, he felt intoxicated by the realization that he had achieved his dream of putting together the best show most of the people in his audiences had ever seen.

Chapter Sixteen

"The Plan" plotted out of hearing range

Regardless of the almost suffocating vigilance of her parents in guarding her from being alone with a man, young or older, Antonella was able occasionally to escape from hearing range while still staying within their sight. That gave her and Rance opportunities to talk briefly about their lives, their hopes, their dreams—and the obstacles they faced in gaining as much control as is humanly possible over the decisions about their futures.

When they first met, Rance had no idea how differently he would be expected to treat Antonella from the way he had related to the girls back home. A subsequent session with Dr. Percy resulted in explanations about different cultures, especially among aristocratic families not only in Mexico but also in many other parts of the world.

Rance listened closely, but he did not understand to his satisfaction. So, the next time he and Antonella were out of hearing distance, he asked her.

"I don't get it, Antonella," he said with some irritation. "Don't your parents trust you? Don't they trust me?"

She giggled like the teenager she was and said candidly: "No, they don't. Honestly, they don't trust me, and they certainly don't trust men, single or married. My parents, and all other parents like them, know about physical attraction and passion, Rance. And I'm pretty sure they know they've seen that you and I are attracted to each other."

"All right," Rance retorted, "but what's so wrong with that? Suppose we had a brief romance? They know you are going home with them as soon as your year's up with us."

"What's wrong is I have to return home a virgin, and I have to stay that way until I am married. Otherwise, in my culture, I am considered 'spoiled goods,' and no respectable man of our class would even consider marrying me. I'd either have to forsake my family and break all ties with them or remain unmarried for life."

"You're joking, Antonella?"

"No, no, no," she said with finality—and almost too loudly, causing both of them to look back at her mother to see if she had heard. "I'm deadly serious, Rance. Believe me. That's the way it is."

"Well, if that's the way it is, how do you ever get to know someone well enough to determine you want to marry him?"

Antonella looked surprised. "Apparently Dr. Percy did not give you the full explanation, Rance," she said, looking deeply and sadly into his eyes. "I probably will have no say in whom I marry. In my culture, parents—especially the father—control that."

"Do you mean your father can pick out your husband and make you marry him?"

"Absolutely. If I am fortunate, I will be pursued by several men my parents will approve of, and I might be able to pick the one I want. But if politics or land or wealth is involved, my parents may use me to the benefit of the whole family and its future.

"Rance, girls my age rarely get to marry for love. Sometimes, if there is reason enough or if people who outrank my father apply enough pressure, my husband may even be an older widower with children as old as I am."

Rance was so shocked, he could think of nothing else to say.

Antonella read his face accurately and disrupted the silence with a statement so blunt and so uncharacteristic for a young woman to make to a young man that both blushed.

"If you think that is so horrible, Rance, can you imagine how I, or any other young girl, would feel having to have sexual relations with an old man like that and having his wrinkled hands and bloated body all over me? It's about the most repulsive thing I can imagine. I not only cry whenever I consider that possibility, I have even thought about ending my life rather than face a fate like that."

"Oh, dear God," Rance rushed to say. "Please run away before you ever do that. You can always come to me, even if it's years from now, and I am married with a bunch of kids, I'll make sure you'll be all right."

"Don't worry, Rance. I want to live. I just want to be happy, too. If that's possible."

* * *

Gradually, over a number of months in which they have other private talks out of hearing range of her mother or her father, they put together a plan that both thrills and frightens them. If they can pull it off, it will be, in their words, "heavenly." If something unforeseen goes wrong, there will be hell to pay.

Even though they haven't yet had a chance to do more than hold hands secretly under the dinner table, they manage to "accidentally" rub against each other while saddling rented horses for brief rides, accompanied at a short distance, of course, by either Alexia or Lorenzo. No matter how much they ache to kiss, they hadn't dared.

Considering all that, their plan is indeed bold. Without discussing the embarrassing details, they determine they will give their virginity to each other if they ever get the chance.

Of course, the plan first and foremost depends upon their ever getting time alone.

Rance is overcome with desire, regardless of how slim the chances are for a rendezvous. Being an American male, he has everything to gain and very little to lose if they are caught. So even though he doesn't want to cause her to change her mind, he asks: "Why are you willing to take such a risk, Antonella?"

"Simply because it is the only way I can make certain my first time will be with a young man I care deeply for. The first time is unforgettable for everyone. It has to be. That's why, for me, it has to be an experience I'll always cherish, especially if I am forced to marry some old man or even a young man I don't want to be with."

Rance has one other worry that also might end up causing Antonella to change her mind. But he asks it out of concern for her welfare and her future. "What if you get pregnant?"

"I thought that through when I was fifteen, Rance. By the grace of God, I was given one aunt who was not traditional in her thinking and was a rebel of sorts in her behavior. She told me in secret precisely the days in each month that I am least likely to conceive. She also told me something a man can do to reduce the risk even more. But it's too embarrassing for me to talk about unless we get to that point."

"God Almighty, Antonella, I want to hold and kiss you so much right now it actually hurts."

"Me, too, Rance. I hope our day will come. And soon. I would pray for it if I weren't worried a wish like that would offend God."

Chapter Seventeen

Rance and Antonella may get their chance

She could not call it divine intervention because she was afraid to pray for this day, but Antonella latched tightly onto an unexpected opportunity for her and Rance to have some safe time alone. But they will have to take the risk of making Abby a co-conspirator for things to work.

A telegram arrived during the eighth month of her family's one-year tenure with the Traveling Sharpshooters Exhibition. It was from Lorenzo's father. At the command of President Porfirio Diaz, Lorenzo's father and mother must attend a state dinner being given by President Grover Cleveland for President Diaz at the White House.

For reasons as yet undisclosed, President Diaz also has requested Lorenzo and Alexia attend as well. Lorenzo knows full well that a request is the same as a command. He has no choice except to attend. And neither does Alexia. Of course, they will take Antonella to Washington with them. It would be unthinkable to allow her to remain behind unchaperoned.

Antonella does not want to go. She sees her parents' absence as perhaps the only chance for her and Rance to put "The Plan" into effect. Antonella has Dr. Percy to thank for trying to persuade her parents to give her permission to remain with the troupe. His motivation was not Antonella and Rance's happiness. He had no idea what they had been planning. Money, pure and simple, was his reason.

"Lorenzo," Dr. Percy had practically begged, "our contracts guarantee Amado and his handlers will be part of the act. Tickets have been sold for this weekend's event, and for the next few weeks as well. We cannot break our word and disappoint the customers. Our reputation might be irreparably damaged.

"I fully understand you and Alexia must attend the dinner. But if you will leave Antonella in our care, I am confident she can do your part in the show — or most of it—as well as her own.

"I give you my word, my friend, that Abby and I will serve as guardians and constant chaperones for your daughter. Believe me, we know how vital that is to you."

"My dear Dr. Percy, I have faith in both you and Abby. But Alexia will not allow it. She will insist on either Antonella going with us or I go alone, and she remain with our daughter. But she cannot stay here. Our president wants to meet with me and Alexia. One does not turn down the president of Mexico. It is impossible."

"May I suggest, Lorenzo, that we have Abby talk with Alexia and try to convince her Antonella will be safe in her care? I have a feeling another woman will have a better chance than a man would in persuading Alexia to permit your daughter to stay with us and perform in the shows. After all, you probably will not be gone long, and trains make traveling much faster these days."

"I'll make an excuse for a luncheon between Abby and my wife," Dr. Percy. "May the gods be with us," Lorenzo's says with a nervous laugh.

* * *

If it had only been her father-in-law, the ambassador, who had "ordered" she be present for some important occasion in Washington, D.C., Alexia would have been as immovable as a mountain in staying with and chaperoning her daughter. But it was the president of Mexico himself. The only way he would excuse her absence would be if she were on her deathbed. And Alexia knew it.

So, after getting a solemn promise from both Abby and Dr. Percy that Abby will provide the same kind of full-time care to Antonella as her mother faithfully did, Alexia extremely reluctantly gave in and accompanied Lorenzo east to attend the state dinner. Alexia, however, did have to admit to herself that she was curious about what her president wanted to talk about with Lorenzo and her.

Rance and Antonella started scheming immediately. They figured their only hope to get some time totally alone depended upon the cooperation of Abby. Dr. Percy, they realized, would be of no help. If Antonella had been an American girl unrestricted by the standards to which Antonella was held, he wouldn't have cared what she and Rance did in private. But there was no way under the sun he would risk his show and especially his financial future to accommodate these two young people.

Chapter Eighteen

Abby is "innocently" manipulated

The show went on, and Antonella pleased Rance, Abby, and especially Dr. Percy by performing flawlessly with Amado, including the part usually attended to by her father. She charmed the crowds not only in leading that strutting horse through his tricks but also with her poise, enchanting smiles, and her beauty.

The others, including Ahiga and Dezba, gave their usual thrilling performances.

Still, just a few days before the return of Lorenzo and Alexia, the young couple had found no way to be out of Abby's and Dr. Percy's sight. Those two gave them more distance than Antonella's parents did, but they were still under watchful eyes that Dr. Percy and Abby had pledged would be vigilant.

Then a turn of events occurred that nagged at Antonella's conscience because of her strict Catholic upbringing, but not enough to keep her from convincing herself that it would be all right to deceive Abby because Abby's own experience would keep her from being fooled.

Dr. Percy received a telegram from the man who had given him, Rance, and Abby the opportunity to risk investing in a promising oil field. Something had happened that the wealthy speculator would talk about only face to face. His time was limited, so he had set the meeting place a two-day round trip away.

"I know I gave my word to your parents," Dr. Percy explained to Antonella, "but I have a feeling a lot of money is to be gained or lost by this opportunity. So, with your permission, I am going to leave you with Abby solely in charge, and you and Rance must promise me two things. First, that you will cooperate fully with Abby, and second that you never, ever tell your parents I was not with you the whole time they were gone.

"Your parents would never forgive or trust me again, and I do not want to lose their respect—or to be completely honest, your horse act."

Everyone agreed and shook hands. Rance's left hand and Antonella's as well were behind their backs with fingers crossed. Not telling her parents would be an easy word to keep. Not trying to manipulate Abby was not part of their bargain.

Antonella lost no time in putting "The Plan" into action. As soon as Dr. Percy had left early the next morning to catch his train, Antonella ordered coffee delivered to the room she and Abby were sharing in her parents' absence. Abby was insightful and experienced in matters of the heart between a young couple obviously excited by the prospect of a loving relationship—no matter how brief.

So she was not at all surprised when she stirred cream and sugar into her coffee and looked across the little table at the young woman whose sparkling eyes belied the words she had practiced and was beginning to deliver.

"Abby," Antonella said with what she hoped was a concerned expression, "I am worried about you."

"Oh, how so?" Abby replied without believing Antonella but looking forward to being amused by whatever scheme her young friend was hatching.

"Well, during the night, you woke me several times with what I think sounds like a cough coming on. Yes, and your breathing was raspy. And I think for the sake of your health and to make sure you will be ready to perform tomorrow night, you should go see a doctor this morning."

"You really think so, Antonella? Did I sound all that bad to you?" Abby was enjoying playing along, but she was going to test Antonella's skills at deception.

"I suppose then that I should send for the hotel's doctor," Abby taunted, knowing that would destroy Antonella's goal.

"No need for that," Antonella quickly responded. "I noticed in one of our walks that there is a doctor's office about ten minutes from the hotel, and I'm sure he has a nurse and more medications on hand than the hotel doctor. Besides, the air might be soothing to your lungs.

"I'll be glad to walk there with you. And Rance can go with us, so we won't be two women alone."

"How long do you think all this will take?" Abby inquired, knowing timing would be of the utmost importance.

"Because you don't have an appointment, I figure you will have to wait about forty-five minutes or so. Then it should take another half hour for them to get your medical history, an additional forty-five minutes for the exam, and if he gives you medication, you will have to stay at least fifteen minutes longer to make sure you do not have a reaction to it."

"So altogether, I'd better allow three hours before you and Rance come back to get me. Right? I know the doctor could finish in less time, but the medication may make me feel too faint to walk back to the hotel by myself."

Abby and Antonella had reached an understanding without either having to admit she was doing anything she should not be. Antonella would have almost three unchaperoned hours with Rance, and Abby had to be able to tell Percy truthfully she went to see a doctor at midday while Antonella and Rance went to check on Amado and pick up their costumes at the laundry.

Abby knew what was at risk, just as Antonella and Rance did. She also knew these two wonderful young virgins stood little chance at even a short-term romance and no possibility of ever marrying. But what helped her convince herself to go along was the horrible and real possibility of Antonella having to marry someone she did not love, especially the skin-crawling prospect that her husband would be a half worn out old man.

Those three hours would give these lovely young people time to make a memory they could cherish and relive the rest of their lives.

Antonella knew all along that Abby would be too perceptive to fall for the excuse Antonella had devised for getting her away for several hours. She also knew her manipulative move would allow Abby to play along and feign innocence.

Abby's justification for breaking her word to never let Antonella out of her sight was simple. Even though her marriage had not worked out, Abby would never forget what it was like to be passionately in love for the first time.

"And I'll be damned if I'll be the one to deny Antonella and Rance their brief moment of intimate joy."

Chapter Nineteen

Riches and bitter-sweet news

True to their word, Rance and Antonella arrived at the doctor's office precisely three hours after they'd last seen Abby. Neither inquired about the status of her health. And neither looked her squarely in her eyes.

Abby, in turn, did not ask about how they had managed their "chores" because there was no need. Antonella and Rance were holding hands, looking a little flushed, and giggling for no apparent reason. That told Abby all she needed to know. She had experienced it all herself years ago but still remembered every detail.

As would Rance and Antonella.

The fact that their lovemaking had been less than expert, even tentative and awkward, was of no matter to them. They quickly learned the art of passionate kissing, tender touching and exploration, and the final coming together each was so eager to experience.

Their eyes had stored a treasure of pictures never to be forgotten. Both were filled with wonder at the sight of the other unclothed. It was a first experience for Antonella. Other than being short in height, Rance had an almost perfectly portioned, muscular, firm body. She was shocked by the size of his arousal and wondered whether she could possibly accommodate him.

The only other mature woman Rance had seen nude was the prostitute he paid to tell him if he was manly adequate. Antonella's wide-eyed look confirmed what the lady of the evening had calculated.

The sight of Antonella took Rance's breath away. He had no inkling the body of a mature young woman could look so very different in the altogether. He was delighted and fascinated by her breasts that were so disproportionately wide that they not only touched in the middle but extended beyond her small body and reigned high and firm above her tiny waist.

Antonella's hips matched her breasts in width, and when Rance compared them to his typical white man's flat behind, he momentarily distracted himself by likening her derriere to two medium-size balloons. Her legs also were rounded at the top and became appealingly slenderer as his eyes moved down them.

Rance put off until last his savoring of Antonella's womanhood. However, its thick, dark covering of curls was unexpectedly expansive. Despite its allure, it seemed to Rance to be almost alien to her other soft, thoroughly feminine, gentle features, sweet face, tiny hands, and soft musical voice. It was, nevertheless, strongly arousing.

What neither Rance nor Antonella would realize until they watched their bodies age over the years was what they were seeing in each other now was the best they would ever look. And the passionate handsomeness of his body and the stunning beauty of her physique would last only a few fleeting years.

That would make their remembrances of the afternoon all the more precious.

* * *

As happy as she was for Rance and Antonella, Abby recognized these two young lovers had no awareness that what they had experienced was evident not only to her, but it also would be to Dr. Percy and to her parents. If for no other reason, it would simply be the different way they were looking at each other.

Abby quickly created a pretext—a reason to hide the real reason. She would privately instruct Rance and Dr. Percy to lavish praise on

Antonella for the superb performances she had given with Amado. Rance might figure out the real reason; Dr. Percy would not, but he was so genuinely pleased with Antonella, he would be delighted to praise her. That, Abby reasoned—and hoped—would provide cover for the blushes and the smiles those two young people would be unable to control for quite some time.

Dr. Percy returned the next day and Lorenzo and Alexia two days later. Both had exciting news. One was for a totally good reason; the other was mixed with sadness.

Dr. Percy could not wait to inform Rance and Abby that their investment of two thousand five hundred dollars and his gamble of ten thousand dollars had paid off tenfold. The company headed by Dr. Percy's friend had struck oil. It was not a deep well, but it had produced enough to return twenty-five thousand dollars each to Rance and Abby and one hundred thousand to Dr. Percy.

This great good fortune put Abby well on her way to the financial independence she desperately wanted and boosted Dr. Percy a huge step closer to the wealthy life and social standing he craved and for which his education had prepared him. As for Rance, who already had saved seven thousand dollars, he could not only raise the standard of living for his family but also provide financial security for himself for years. The ten thousand dollars was equal to the annual pay of at least thirty-five cowboys.

The Guerreros' news was bitter-sweet. President Diaz presented Lorenzo with the honor of a new, very important position. He was appointing Lorenzo to First Secretary of the Diplomatic Corps. Lorenzo would not be appointing diplomats or instructing them on how to do their jobs. That was President Diaz's exclusive privilege. But Lorenzo would be in charge of managing virtually everything else: hiring support personnel for both at home and abroad, and providing all equipment, supplies, and meeting any other needs of the corps.

It was a huge promotion. A great honor. Lorenzo and Alexia were pleased, but even if they hadn't been, there was no way the offer could have been declined.

That was the sweet part. The bitter aspect was that the Guerreros would have only three weeks, including travel time, to wrap up their arrangement with Dr. Percy and report to Mexico City.

Dr. Percy had lost a valuable act and a lucrative part of his show. The loss of the popular horse act would mean a reduction in the price he could command from the promoters who ran the arenas in which his troupe performed. But to give the money-hungry professor the credit he deserved, he also liked the Guerreros personally and would miss their company.

Abby shared Dr. Percy's feelings, and for mostly the same reasons. She would miss her growing relationship with Antonella, and she would worry about the effect Antonella's absence would have on Rance. Would he revert to his sulky behavior, or worse, would he sink into a genuine depression? The show could not go on without him.

As for Antonella and Rance, the news was devastating. They knew from the beginning that their relationship would be limited, but they had tried to put that out of their minds until the year was up. Now that time was being cut short.

Within a year, Antonella likely would be married to Lord-knows-who, and Rance had no prospects for doing anything other than displaying his skills with a pistol.

There was little to no chance they would ever see each other again.

Chapter Twenty

The homecoming and its surprises

Rance and Antonella could not even promise to write to each other. Although she might be able to risk sending mail to him, they could figure no way for Rance to confidentially send her letters. She would have no address of her own, and she had no confidant in Mexico City. Her one aunt she trusted lived too far away, and they would seldom see each other.

Perhaps over time, Antonella would make a friend she would trust. But her friends undoubtedly would live with their parents, too, or have a spouse who might open and read their letters. Although it broke her heart, Antonella begged Rance to accept their fate, and for both of their sakes never try to contact her again.

Feeling the hopelessness of youth, whose inexperience with the ecstasy and the agony of first love fools them into thinking they will never love again, Rance tried to shut himself off from the world—just as Abby had feared. He sank deeply into the "haze," a condition in which he could think only of one aspect of life, the part he felt was the *only* part worth living.

He wanted to be with Antonella—even to the exclusion of his profession, his ties to Abby and to Dr. Percy, his commitment to their show—just everything. He was consumed, and he didn't know what to do about it.

At the risk of losing Rance altogether, Dr. Percy and Abby came up with the only solution they could hope would help. While they tried to find some kind of a replacement act for the Guerreros and Amado, they needed to give Rance some time to re-evaluate his life and envision it in a more optimistic context. So, they suggested he go home and visit his family he hadn't seen in more than two years.

Surprisingly, Rance agreed, and purchased tickets for train travel that would get him to Mabscott with only a couple of overnight stops. He packed two suitcases full of his nice clothes but dressed in his "farm boy outfit" to reduce the chances he would be recognized from his shooting performances he had given widely throughout the West. He had gotten a lot of publicity, and his picture had been on hundreds of posters attached to windows and buildings for hundreds of miles.

His mood brightened at the prospect of seeing his mother and his dad and both siblings. Taylor was sixteen now, and she probably had changed the most of any of them. His folks had told him many times about how famous he had become in their community. He would be greeted warmly.

* * *

The moment he sees his family—all of whom have gathered at the train station to greet him—Rance feels two unanticipated emotions. His heart rises from dark depression to genuine joy, and he feels shamefully guilty about being away from his loved ones for too long.

His father and his brother rush to give him big bear hugs and carry his suitcases while his mother and his sister wait eagerly for their reunion. Taylor, who looks much more like a woman than the little girl he last saw, hugs him warmly. Rance is surprised she has tears in her eyes, causing his heart to sink a little lower in guilt. But it was Rance himself who was shocked when tears filled his eyes with the powerful, almost desperate embrace from his mother.

"I'm proud of you, son. You've been faithful about staying in touch, but I've longed to see you and touch you again."

The women spread the table with every kind of good food Rance always favored: chicken fried crisp and topped with a thick, spicy gravy, creamy mashed potatoes, garden tomatoes, corn on the cob, green beans, and hot cloverleaf rolls with freshly churned butter.

The meal is polished off with the cake Rance always requested his mother make for his birthday: four alternate layers of white and chocolate cake topped by fluffy white icing that also is placed between each layer.

"Mother, Taylor, this is the best meal and biggest treat I've had since I left Mabscott. And for the next couple of days, I'm gonna eat every bite of the leftovers. You went to a lot of trouble. Just want you to know this means a lot."

Everyone joins in to clear the table, but when the men have provided about all the help she can put up with, Fanny shoos them out of the kitchen while she and Taylor finish the cleaning.

When they join the men in the sitting room, they bring coffee and pull their chairs closely together and stare at Rance with grins that puzzle him. Rance can feel his folks are up to something that, at the moment, completely eludes him. Until Fanny and Taylor produce a large package decorated in fancy paper and ribbons.

Rance just smiles and handles it gently, concerned it might be something fragile.

"Well, open it!" Taylor orders impatiently.

Rance moves slowly, taking care not the rip the pretty paper or damage the expensive ribbons. "Get on with it, son," Patterson almost shouts, hardly able to wait to see Rance's reaction.

It is a shirt the women have made for him. But not just any nice shirt. It is decorated in the western designs Rance performs in. They used the photos he has sent as their guide. It is a bright yellow embroidered in a variety of colors with horses, bison, cacti, and pistols. Rance knows absolutely nothing about sewing, but he recognizes his mother and his sister have put many hours of work into this surprise gift. He lavishes them with praise.

Then looking expectantly at his father and Tyrone, Rance jokes: "Well, what did the two of you sew for me?" He was kidding, not expecting anything else on top of the wonderful meal and his shirt, which he tells them he will wear proudly in his most important performances.

"We didn't sew you nothin', Mr. Sharpshooter," Tyrone retorts. "But we have a little package for you, too." Patterson walks into his and Fanny's bedroom and returns carrying with both hands a package smaller than Fanny and Taylor's gift. It is wrapped simply in brown paper, and it is much heavier than the prettier package.

Rance opens it and is speechless. His dad and his brother have made him the most intricately engraved pistol he has ever seen. Its size is perfect for a fast draw. Its weight and balance are precise, and it has the same kind of sculpted ivory handles Patterson had made him before to keep his gun from slipping in his sweaty hands during a performance on a hot day.

"It will fit the way you want into the two holsters you already have," Patterson explains. "We didn't make you a new holster because we realized the others are broken in to your liking and fit the way you want on your side and tied down to your leg.

"While you're here, you can give that pistol a workout in our shooting range to see if it needs any adjusting," Tyrone says. "But we don't think it will."

"I can't wait," Rance replies enthusiastically. "First thing in the morning.

"But now let me show you what I have brought you. You probably wondered why I hauled two suitcases along for such a brief stay. Well, let me get one from my bedroom and open it for you.

86

Inside are bracelets for the women. They are handmade works of art fashioned out of silver and turquoise stones by Navajo friends of Ahiga and Dezba. Fanny and Taylor put them on admiringly, and they are obviously pleased.

"I made the right choice, I guess?"

"Are you kidding?" Taylor all but shouts. "I'm sleeping with mine on my wrist tonight."

Fanny gives her son a warm hug and beams. "I've never seen a prettier bracelet."

Patterson's and Tyrone's gifts are in much bigger boxes. Inside are hand tooled western boots, precise copies of the ones Dr. Percy had made for Rance. A deep brown with an ivory pistol design on the side.

Ever the businessman, Rance's dad proclaims: "Rance, these are not only beautiful boots, but they make good advertisement for our gun business."

"Thanks, brother," Tyrone says while giving Rance a couple of good pounds on the shoulder. "I'll show these off all over town."

For the remainder of the evening, Rance's family hears at their demand every detail about his career, his triumphs and all the good and the bad points about his experience as a traveling exhibitionist sharpshooter. Rance complies, imitating Dr. Percy's skills in exaggerating all the parts Rance knows they want to hear, whether they are completely truthful or not.

He does not tell them about his feelings for Antonella or Abby and the happiness and heartbreak each has given him. He also does not mention the money he made in the oil venture. He wants to take a while to observe how he can use some of his money to make his folks' lives easier and happier.

Rance is able for the first time in recent memory to be at peace with himself and his life. The loss of Antonella still hurts deeply, but thoughts of her do not dominate this night. His unrequited desire for Abby remains painful but also mostly out of his mind for a while. Whether his career as a sharpshooter exhibitionist will be long or brief is a decision he can put off for a time. For right now, he is home. In the bed he slept in for years. Surrounded by family who love him unconditionally, who support him, and who are both joyful and grateful to have him home.

He slips into a restful, peaceful sleep.

Chapter Twenty-One

Rance's life-changing gift

Two days before Rance must take a train to rejoin the Traveling Sharp-shooters Exhibition, he talks at dinner about all the changes made in Mabscott while he has been gone.

"Two new saloons, I see, mother. How do all the women at our church feel about that?"

"We're not happy about that, I can assure you," Fanny affirms. "We sure didn't need any more drunks and crime. But at least we had some say about their locations. They're nowhere near our churches, our schools, and our best shops."

"Did you notice the old livery stable has been rebuilt and expanded?" Tyrone asks.

"I did. Big improvement," Rance responds.

Patterson and Taylor go over a few other points while Rance listens patiently. He wasn't as interested as he had made himself seem to be. He was working up to something. After diverting everyone's attention to all the other changes, he mentions to his mother in what he hopes sounds casual a certain house she has always admired.

It was built on the outskirts of town by the late bank owner, Grant Logan. It is a white two-story structure built in the Victorian style with lots of intricate gingerbread trim that gives it the look of a giant version of a dollhouse.

"When I walked by it the other day, it seemed to be vacant, mother. Is no one livin' there now?"

"No, honey. It's not occupied. Mr. Logan's widow, Brooke, has it up for sale, furnishings and all because she has moved to St. Louis where she has a married daughter and two grandchildren. But it's expensive, so it hasn't gotten any offers even though she has reduced the price. Or at least that's what I hear."

"Think the person handlin' the sale will let us get a tour of it, mother?"

"Well, I was going to say I doubt it because he knows we don't have the money to buy it. But, then again, he just might. He has become a big fan of yours, what with all the publicity you've been getting. He's mentioned to me and your father several times he'd like to get your autograph and hear about your experiences. I think you remember him, Jackson Barbour. He was about three years ahead of you in school, and he's a lawyer now."

"Yeah, I know who he is. Want me to go see him and find out if I can set somethin' up?"

"Oh, I'd love to have a tour, son. As you know, we didn't run in Mr. Logan's circles, so we were never invited to any of the social gatherings he and his wife had in that house. Just hope the Lord will forgive me for all the envy I'm going to feel if I get to walk through it."

* * *

Rance set it up. Jackson made it easy for him to ask the favor.

"It'll cost you an autograph, Rance. And," he added with a self-serving chuckle, "I wouldn't mind a brief personal note I can make people envious with, especially when I'm traveling on business."

"Done," said Rance. "I'd like to take you to lunch, if you have the time, Jackson."

"Putting on my coat right now, Rance. Just give me a second to tell my secretary where I'll be."

Being close in age and therefore having a lot in common, the two get so comfortable with each other that the mid-day meal of cornbread and bean soup stretches beyond an hour. Jackson suggested Rance and his family meet him right after five o'clock when both his office and the gun shop close.

Rance decided to walk to the livery stable to rent a nice carriage so the family could ride in a finer style than in their buckboard. Jackson told him the man who ran the stables had a nice one he rented out.

He didn't tell Rance who that man was. Turned out to be one hell of a shock.

The livery stable was attached to a blacksmith shop, and when the big man hammering away on a wagon wheel rim turned around, it was none other than Rance's old tormentor and nemesis, Bruno Buttus. Genuine surprise spread immediately across both men's faces.

"Well, I'll be damned if it ain't the man with the big gun!" Bruno blurted out.

"Oh, shit," Rance said regretfully to himself. "Of all the people in Mabscott to run into, it had to be old pig nose. Wonder if he still hates me?"

Bruno's outstretched rough and dirty hand relieved Rance's apprehension.

"Good to see you, Rance. I would say you look all grown up, but I've seen so many pictures and posters of you, it's no surprise to me. You're famous, boy. The whole damn town's proud of you."

Rance reached out and shook Bruno's big, strong hand, and joked: "Glad you're using that hand to shake mine instead of punching me with it, Bruno. My God; if anything, that grip tells you've gotten even a lot stronger."

Bruno boomed a pleasurable laugh at the compliment.

"Rance, I've turned my thinking around since we were in school. Would you believe I got married a year out of high school and have a baby girl?"

"That's great, Bruno. But to be honest, I couldn't be more surprised. How'd all this come about?"

"Well, a new family moved into town. Had a girl, Sally, about my age, and we hit it off. By some miracle she took to me, and because no other girl had ever had anything to do with me, I jumped at the chance to have a girlfriend. Six months later, we were married. I was working as an apprentice to a blacksmith, so my dad and my father-in-law got together and bought the stable and the blacksmith shop as a wedding present for Sally and me.

"Life is good, Rance, but it would be even better if you could manage to accept my apologies for the way I treated you. I regret it, and if there's anything I can do for you to make up for it, you just say the word."

"Actually, there is something. I came here hoping to rent that nice carriage Jackson Barbour said you have."

"Absolutely, Rance. When do you want it?"

"Right now. To use this afternoon, if that's possible."

"Sure it is. Just give me fifteen minutes or so to wipe the dust off it and hitch up a good horse."

"That's great, Bruno," Rance said as he reached into his pocket and pulled out some money.

"No charge," Bruno said with finality. "I'm just real happy to get to do this for you and your family."

* * *

Riding in the grand carriage was a new experience for the Cabells—all but Fanny, that is. She had been reared in a family that enjoyed this kind of luxury. Their house also had been as fine as the one they were about to tour.

Rance was eager to look at the house and its furnishings, too, but mostly he wanted to watch his mother closely to see if the memories this estate would reawaken in her would be pleasing or would make her sad for the life she once knew. He pretty much already knew what his father's and his siblings' reactions would be. They would admire the house and its expensive furnishings, but it would be more like window shopping in a big city where they could only admire but not afford anything.

The mansion was not huge like those extremely wealthy families built in New York or Chicago or places like that. But it did have five large bedrooms with canopied beds, high decorative posts, and side curtains to let in the night air while warding off insects. A spectacular curved staircase connected the first and second floors.

Lavish furnishings included heavy, dark, decorative furniture with lush upholstery in reds, greens, violets and magenta. A few stained-glass windows. A couple of elaborate chandeliers. Large ornate mirrors. Voluminous draperies. Rugs of rich colors and floral patterns. A spacious, fully furnished kitchen.

Patterson, Taylor, and Tyrone spent most of the tour joking about how rich people lived and giving way to exaggerated oohings and aahings, wondering how it would feel to actually live in such surroundings.

"Fanny," Patterson teased, "I bet you'd make all of us take off our shoes in that big old entrance way and confine us to eatin' in the kitchen or the dinin' room."

Fanny smiled politely but said little. She answered more with nods and smiles. It was obvious to Rance's observing eyes the tour had transported her back into another time and place—a time and place in which she had lived until she married a wonderful man with an ordinary income. She had never regretted marrying Patterson. She loved him and her children as dearly as was humanly possible. Still, it would have been nice not having to give up so many advantages.

While the men checked out the carriage house out back and inspected the four acres of grounds on which the house sat, Fanny and Taylor ran their hands admiringly over the furniture, the fixtures, the draperies, and the thick rugs. Taylor was in awe; Fanny allowed her mind to imagine the "what ifs" that intrigue every human, especially as the years separate them farther and farther away from their youth.

With the tour at an end, the family gathered in the entrance to thank Jackson for the privilege of having a leisurely look at a magnificent house.

For some reason unknown to all the others except Rance, Jackson fumbles with the front door, as if he is having trouble opening it. Then patting his pockets theatrically, he "finds" the key in his vest pocket. His physical actions have gotten everyone's attention, so with all of them looking to see what the problem is, he turns to Fanny and extends his hand holding the key.

"I believe this belongs to you, Mrs. Cabell."

"Me?" she responds. "Oh, no, Jackson. I have my house key right here in my pocketbook. You better keep looking for the key to lock this house."

"But this key does now belong to you and your family," Mrs. Cabell. "You've owned the place since 1 o'clock this afternoon."

* * *

As the entire family hugs him goodbye at the train station and waves as it chugs away from Mabscott, Rance ponders whether people live more than one life over the course of a lifetime. Sadness tugs at his heart as he separates himself once again from one life he lives in his hometown with his loving family, his longtime friends, and all the connections and memories he has back to the day he was born, and transforms into his other very different life as a professional sharpshooter who puts his skills on display for money.

He is secure in the love and happiness he will always have in Mabscott, but he isn't at all certain how long his professional life will last or even whether he and Dr. Percy and Abby will eventually part, never to see one another again.

Anyway, he'll be in Santa Fe soon for the next show. "I can just pick up where I left off," he figures.

The return trip was uneventful.

Until he departed the train and took that fateful step into the saloon in Santa Fe.

Chapter Twenty-Two

Loving support

As he predicted, Rance has a restless night as the sheriff's guest at the jail. He has managed to sleep off and on a little, but try as he may, he can't stop his mind from dwelling on the killing of Kodiak only a few hours earlier. Nevertheless, Rance stays as quiet as he can until the sheriff awakens and starts stirring around.

"Did you get any shut-eye last night, son?" the sheriff asks as Rance joins him in the office.

"Not much, sir. Guess it's gonna take a good while to clear my head and get back to normal again."

"That will happen, Rance. Take my word for it. As I told you last night, shootin' that no good asshole saved a lot of lives. Take comfort in that.

"Feel up to eatin' a little breakfast?"

"I'm not sure about that, sheriff. But I do want to treat you to a meal for your thoughtfulness in letting me bunk in the jail and for sharin' your experiences with me about getting' over a shootin'.

"I think I'll first check into the hotel where my troupe has reservations. You want to meet in the hotel restaurant in about fifteen minutes?"

"I gotta better idea, son. Granny Sprague's Café's got the best food in town by far. When you see how big and fluffy her biscuits are, I think you'll get your appetite back. I'll walk over to the hotel with you. Granny's place is just up the street from there."

* * *

By the time Dr. Percy, Abby, Ahiga, and Dezba arrive at the hotel in the afternoon, the news of the previous night's gun fight has spread far and wide, causing considerable excitement in the town. Rance's friends heard about it as soon as they got off the train. It's just about all anyone is talking about.

When they spot Rance in the lobby, Abby rushes to him first and wraps her arms tightly around him and doesn't let go.

"Oh, Rance. Thank God you're not hurt. Are you sure you're all right?"

"Physically, I'm fine," he reassures Abby and the others. "Mentally, I'm going to struggle with this for a while."

Dr. Percy also feels great relief. First, because he sincerely cares about Rance. But being the excellent businessman and promotor he is, Dr. Percy is immediately aware that the four shows—two on Friday and two more Saturday—will be sellouts. Everybody will want to see in action the small sharpshooter who slew the giant standing more than a foot taller and weighing three times as much. Dr. Percy's only concern was whether Rance's aim will be overshadowed by his guilt over killing a man.

Meanwhile, Dr. Percy has details and arrangements to be completed. So, he shifts everyone's attention back to their upcoming shows. "Let's get settled in our rooms, have some lunch, then get in a practice session at the exhibition grounds. I'm told the place is within walking distance."

Dezba takes her turn at hugging Rance warmly. She surprises him by pulling him gently aside, out of hearing distance of the others. She has wise and consoling words for Rance because her experiences in her married life with her warrior husband give her the intuition to know Rance can find some solace in what she has to reveal.

"Rance," Dezba says softly while still holding him and her face within inches of his, "I have seen on my husband the look you have on your face. Truly I know what you are going through and what you are feeling. So, I am going to tell you what I told Ahiga years ago when he was a young warrior fighting not only white soldiers but also Indians from other tribes.

"When you must fight to the death even though you would much prefer to live in peace and do no harm, you should feel no shame or guilt if you kill with honor. Ahiga has killed many men, but always with honor. You've known him long enough to know that he is a gentle soul by choice, treats others with respect, makes friends with all who will accept his friendship, and lives a happy life with me. For the sake of the good life you deserve, you must do likewise."

As she pulls away from Rance, Ahiga puts a strong arm around Rance's shoulders, smiles knowingly and says: "I think I have knowledge of what my Dezba has said to you. She has wisdom, Rance. She speaks the truth."

* * *

As usual, the astute Dr. Percy is correct in predicting the positive effect the shooting has in attracting huge, enthusiastic crowds to the performances. Everyone wants to get a good look at Rance in action. Even Dr. Percy did not anticipate the standing ovation Rance got just by walking into the arena. Apparently, Kodiac had no admirers, much less friends. Many feared him; no one liked him.

To them, Rance is a genuine hero.

The performances go well. Abby's aim is perfect, and the spectators, as always, admire her skill and greatly enjoy her shooting the cigar out of the "reluctant" Dr. Percy's mouth.

Ahiga, as always, scares the hell out of them, both with his fierce look and his aggressive attack with tomahawks and lances on his beautiful princess wife.

Unfortunately, they do not get the pleasure and fun of seeing Lorenzo and Antonella perform with Amado. They have already moved to Mexico City.

Rance finds, as many troubled people do, that giving full concentration to a task helps temporarily take their minds off what is disturbing them. The standing ovation, the continual applause, and the spectators' awe at seeing his speed and accuracy in handling his pistol captures all of Rance's attention. He is able to shoot with the same accuracy he always does.

Which is a relief not only to him, but also to his fellow performers, and especially to Dr. Percy, whose ears hear loudly and clearly the clinking of coins dropping in great numbers into his coffers.

Chapter Twenty-Three

The Sharpshooters' future is in doubt

Dr. Percy was uncharacteristically worried. Not about money. His troupe was bringing in plenty of that. He was concerned the Traveling Sharpshooters Exhibition he had so carefully put together was about to fall apart.

Lorenzo and his family and their immensely popular horse act were gone, never to return. Ahiga and Dezba informed him they would leave at the end of the current season. And despite his flawless performance after the killing of Kodiak, Rance obviously was emotionally unstable.

Ahiga and Dezba felt isolated. Because they were Indians, they didn't even have the freedom to shop, dine, or even walk the streets of most towns in which they performed. It wasn't so bad when they had their close friends, the Guerreros, with whom to associate. They liked Abby, Rance, and Dr. Percy, but it wasn't the same because they all had separate lives to live. No, Ahiga and Dezba wanted to be back with their own Navajo people, traveling and performing in a small circuit close to their home base. The greater money they were making with Dr. Percy wasn't worth it anymore.

With only Rance and Abby, the group no longer would be the head-liners at the shows, which meant no two-a-day performances and much less income. Dr. Percy already had accumulated almost one hundred seventy-five thousand dollars. A fortune to most people, but nowhere near what the ambitious former college professor needed to find his place among society's elite.

Meanwhile, the group would be together for three more months be-fore their season ended, so Dr. Percy still had time to try to find replacements for his Indian and Mexican friends. Question was, could he locate two other groups that would come up to the standards of the unique acts he lost?

To add more excitement and to garner more attention, Dr. Percy consulted with Rance and Abby about putting more emphasis on challenges from audience members who believed they had special shooting talents, too. Because neither Rance nor Abby had ever lost a challenge, Dr. Percy said he was willing to step up the challenge money from triple to quadruple. He would offer two hundred dollars against any challenger's fifty. To speed things up to provide time for more challenges, Dr. Percy would require everyone challenging Rance to compete at the same time. Same for Abby's competitors.

Dr. Percy's gamble, as usual, paid off handsomely. Neither of his sharpshooters lost a single match—until complications set in when they were performing in Houston in their last exhibition of the season, where they once again ran up against a sore loser.

An old former buffalo hunter would not accept that he could be beaten by a woman. The consequences were disastrous.

* * *

Abby and Dr. Percy had recognized the change in Rance immediately after they joined him in Santa Fe to resume their show after he killed Kodiac. Rance seemed to transform without any transition from a boy on the edge of manhood into an adult.

It wasn't that he didn't laugh anymore or joke around or enjoy the competitive challenges. But he had become more serious, more pensive, keeping more within himself.

Nobody quite put it into words, but what it amounted to was Rance had lost all of his boyhood innocence. Killing a man had robbed him of that pleasant period in his life.

Before his unwanted encounter with Kodiak—which he had done everything in his power to avoid by admitting before witnesses that Kodiak could beat him with fists or a gun—Rance had never even thought about taking someone's life away from him. Not even if that person was a remorseless menace to every decent citizen who was innocently walking down the street.

Nobody who had killed another human being could ever truly feel carefree again.

Nevertheless, Rance had been forced into such an action, and it changed him in one more significant way that took some time for him to realize. From that fateful day forward, Rance Cabell resolved never again to tolerate a bully. Regardless of whether he or someone else was the person being harassed.

What that buffalo hunter and his ruthless cohort did to Abby three months later pushed Rance over the edge of his control.

He resolved to intervene—even if it meant killing again.

* * *

Rance stared without moving his eyes from Abby for a long, long time. What started as anger rapidly built into barely controlled rage. He had been mad many times before. At his siblings. His parents. His teachers. Especially Bruno Buttus, who had bullied him throughout elementary school.

But he had never before been furious. Especially to the point that he felt like killing.

He could not take his eyes off Abby's bandages as she lay in bed at the doctor's office drugged to escape the pain in her right hand from having every knuckle, her thumb, and all of her fingers busted, broken, and mangled by the challenger she had thoroughly embarrassed on purpose in yesterday's performance. After losing to her, he had loudly berated her in front of the audience, accusing her of being a man disguised as a woman because "no damned titless female could possibly outshoot a real man."

When he dared her to "drop your drawers and prove you are really a woman," Abby was so provoked she shot his hat right off his head and fired bullets so close to his feet, he broke into a clumsy dance to protect his toes.

Enraged and red-faced with shame, he kicked up a big fuss as two deputy sheriffs Dr. Percy had hired just in case they were needed dragged him to jail to cool off. The deputies warned Dr. Percy to keep an eye on Abby until the two men left town because the one he identified as Raleigh Putnam kept muttering threats all the way to the jail.

"Might nothin' come of it," Deputy Clay Hancock said. "But best you be on the lookout. Never can tell whether somebody like that will calm down or try to get revenge."

However, looking after Abby was no small feat. She promised she'd never venture from their wagons or the hotel without a fully loaded rifle. "But you are not going to babysit me. And I'm not hiding in my room with nothing to do when we're not performing," she declared. "If he messes with me, I'll put enough holes in him that the wind will whistle right through his shirt without making so much as a ruffle."

Nobody doubted Abby's ability to protect herself out in the open, especially against one man. But this hombre had cohorts. And it was pretty darned clear from his outbursts and threats that he didn't live by the civilized standards of fair play.

Abby was not foolish. She was not going to venture out after dark. But she felt safe walking in the afternoon to the general store down the street to look at some clothing. She was carrying her rifle in her shooting hand with the barrel pointed to the ground, both for safety and to keep her from looking dangerous to fellow shoppers.

Regardless, Abby did not see what was coming when Raleigh Putnam jerked her into a narrow alley between buildings, stuffed a rag into her mouth, and beat her into a state of semi-consciousness. Then to give her the worst punishment and the most pain he and Madison Wetzel could think of for a person who made a living as a sharpshooter, they held her wrist against the brick side of a building, took her own rifle, and repeatedly slammed the metal-tipped butt against every part of her right hand—her shooting hand.

The entire attack took only a few minutes, and when they had satisfied themselves they had ruined her hand, they left her unconscious and bleeding, walked slowly to their horses and rode out of town in a calm manner that would attract no attention. By the time Abby would be able to talk and identify them, they would have a head start no posse could easily overcome.

Rance did not know the first thing about tracking—reading hoof prints, evaluating horse droppings, checking for broken tree branches, and determining from campfire ashes how long ago the site had been used.

But two things he did know convinced him he could find the two men who had so cruelly abused Abby: He knew their names, and he had seen their faces. In addition, Morgan Summers, the man who ran the livery stable, described in detail the horses they were riding. Rance had plenty of money. He could afford to stay on their trail indefinitely.

"I'll damn sure find them," he pledged to himself. "And when I do, I'll damn sure make them pay."

The only reason he had not already gotten on their trail was staying long enough to check on Abby and having a chance to comfort her. But the longer he waited, the farther away Raleigh Putnam and Madison Wetzel would ride.

Abby was drugged to help her handle the otherwise intolerable pain, so Rance left her a note, promising to find the men and return to her as soon as he could.

He bought a compass, a territorial map, and the best horse and saddle Morgan Summers had for sale. Marion Gilmer, who owned the general store, put together the supplies his experience told him Rance needed for the long miles between towns.

"Good luck," Dr. Percy said when Rance rode by the hotel to say goodbye. "I'll take good care of Abby. Don't you worry yourself any about that, my friend."

"I won't, Dr. Percy. I couldn't leave Abby in any better hands than yours."

Rance needed his friend there. With his big city background, Dr. Percy would be more of a hindrance than a help if he accompanied Rance.

As ill equipped and as inexperienced as he was for tracking criminals, Rance was on his own.

Chapter Twenty-Four

To capture or to kill?

Everybody—including Deputy Clay Hancock, Dr. Percy, and the store-keeper who outfitted Rance—advised him to let the law find and arrest Putnam and Wetzel.

"Let me send out telegrams to law officers in every direction," Hancock suggested. "We have physical descriptions, their names, and what their horses look like. Those two have to get supplies and their whiskey somewhere. They'll surely be recognized."

"I know that makes good sense," Rance countered, "but I can't tolerate just waiting here. I've got to be after them, as illogical as that sounds. But, Clay, I will send you telegrams from every town I'm in, and you can let me know if they've been arrested or at least seen by someone who noticed what direction they were headed in."

And with those words, Rance was off toward Rock Lick, fifty miles south.

Even though Rance was reared in the middle of a small town, he nevertheless was a city boy. He slept indoors, ate food made and served by others, and had never gutted a fish or a squirrel and prepared it for cooking over an open fire. And while tucked snuggly into a warm bed with a comfortable quilt cover, he'd never had to worry about being sneaked up on by a rattlesnake or a wolf.

Traveling from town to town was going to be mighty unpleasant for him.

By the time he got to Rock Lick, his butt ached, his back and shoulders hurt, and he was in the foul mood that always set in when he'd gone too long without a decent meal. As hungry as he was, however, he first checked in at the sheriff's office, where he was greeted in a friendly manner by Nicholas Monroe.

"Call me Nick," the sheriff said after Rance introduced himself. "So, you're lookin' for someone. Well, if he's a local, I'll know him, and if he's a stranger, I've either seen him or been told who he is and why he's in town. Like to keep up with things, son. I've made that my business for more years than you've been alive."

"Well, that's good to know, sheriff. Let me tell you why I'm looking for them and what they and their horses look like."

"Sorry, Rance," Nick said after listening closely. "Nobody like that has passed through here. But I can tell you where they'd most likely go if they think somebody's after them, and they're on the run."

"That would be helpful, sheriff. I'm listening."

"My guess is those galoots had enough provisions to travel about a hundered miles. So, if they have a lick of sense, they'd likely skip all the little towns and head for the biggest one about that distance away. Less likely they would draw attention in a bigger place."

"And what would that place be, sir?"

"Beards Fork, about fifty miles southwest of here, Rance. They have a good supply store there, and a few saloons and a couple of places where women are available for a price. Those two no-goods you're after probably spend a considerable amount of time in both places.

"I can give you directions over breakfast, if you're hungry."

"Sheriff, left to my own devices on the trail, I would probably starve. I'm so hungry I could eat the south end of a northbound polecat," Rance grinned.

Nick laughed out loud. "Sassy's Café has food that sure as hell better than that. C'mon, boy, and let's get you a good meal before you set off."

* * *

Conflicting thoughts ran through Rance's mind as he rode off to Beards Fork. He had had time to become a little more coolheaded than he was when his thoughts and actions turned furious when he first saw the bloody bandages covering Abby's ruined gun hand. His hatred for Raleigh and Madison at that moment would have meant their instant death had they been in range of his pistol at the moment.

Now, he was pondering what he would do when he caught up with them. Maybe he would not kill them. Perhaps if they were willing to surrender peacefully, he would let the law take its course. But what course would that likely be?

At most, they might plead guilty or be found guilty by a jury of maiming and other such charges. The sentence probably would be less than five years in prison. If only a couple of years, Raleigh and Madison might be allowed to serve that time in the local jail.

Wouldn't do Abby any good to sue those worthless bums for pain, suffering, and lost income both for the present and the future. Those sorry drifters each owned nothing more than a horse, a saddle, a pistol and a rifle, one pair of boots, and a couple of shirts and pants. Suing would be a waste of time.

"Call that justice!

"Hell no," Rance concluded. "That's nowhere near enough. That's too easy."

If they would not initiate a gunfight when Rance caught up with them, should he? That would give him all the excuse he needed for killing them both and doing every other living person a favor. What good did those two whiskey-swilling, whore-hopping bullies ever do to justify their right to live among decent people?

Thinking about all of these possibilities made Rance feel a mite better because punishing somebody in his own mind didn't make him feel guilty. After all, he hadn't carried any of it out. What it all boiled down to, he reasoned, was his parents had reared him and his siblings to respect everything God had given life. He had been given no choice in killing Kodiak, so he had peace of mind about its justification. But he could not kill Raleigh and Madison without giving them a chance to surrender. God would not forgive that, Rance just knew.

With his mind occupied, at least the trip went faster, and he got through all the dreaded camping, cooking, and sleeping outdoors. "Good thing I never wanted to be a cowboy or a lawman chasing criminals for a living. Give me a good home-cooked meal and a cozy bed inside of a warm bedroom any day."

Beards Fork wasn't much of a town, but it was, as the sheriff had described, large enough to give travelers a place to rest overnight and resupply their needs. So, to follow the dictates of his conscience, Rance checked in first thing at the sheriff's office.

It was locked with a note saying the sheriff would be back about 1 p.m. That was just an hour, so Rance decided to sit in one of the chairs the sheriff and his deputies kept on the wooden sidewalk outside the office. The sheriff's name, Ritchie Wood, was carved neatly above the door handle.

The street wasn't too busy at noon on a Tuesday. A few men on horses, a farmer and his family riding a buckboard loaded with crops to sell, probably at the general store. A couple of men who walked by and acknowledged his presence by saying howdy. A woman and her small daughter carrying packages.

Ordinary people doing ordinary things on an ordinary day in an ordinary town.

A big middle-aged man with a bushy black beard started Rance's way from across the street. He was wearing a badge and had two guns strapped around his waist. His whole demeanor gave the impression he meant business to any stranger unfamiliar to him.

"You waitin' on me, mister?" he inquired in a neutral tone, neither friendly nor unfriendly.

"Yessir," Rance replied respectfully, getting to his feet and offering his hand to the big man. He had a strong grip and a brief handshake.

"C'mon in and tell me what I can do for you. Rance, did you say your name was?"

"That's right, sheriff," Rance said, taking the seat Wood pointed toward.

"I'm looking for two outlaws. But my reason will take a little explanation, if you've got the time right now."

"You a bounty hunter?" the sheriff asked with obvious dislike.

"No, sir."

"A lawman, then?"

"Not that either, sheriff. Actually, I am a member of a group called the Traveling Sharpshooters Exhibition, and I'm looking for two men who took a rifle butt and smashed the shooting hand of our lady sharpshooter, who, by the way, is a first cousin of Annie Oakley." Rance thought dropping that famous name might help him warm up his cause with the sheriff.

"Tell me about it, Rance. You have my full attention."

So Rance did, giving the sheriff the names and descriptions of Raleigh and Madison, as well as their horses.

"What makes you think they might be here in Beards Fork?"

"Only that it would make sense for them to need supplies considering how long they've been on the road. Besides, I'm told they can't stay away from whiskey and whores long enough to have traveled much farther."

The sheriff chuckled at that remark, and then said something that took Rance by surprise.

"I think I just saw two men fittin' that description over in the saloon. They were drinkin' and playin' cards. Not causin' any trouble, but I noticed them in particular because they were loud and messin' around with a couple of the girls."

"Have I given you enough information to arrest them, sheriff?"

"I think so, if you are willing to swear out a warrant, which I take for granted you are. But I may have to run a bluff to get to keep them in jail until the traveling judge gets here next week."

"That would be perfect, sheriff. I must say I did not expect to catch up with them so soon. How do you want to handle their arrest?"

"You a sharpshooter with that fancy pistol you're wearin', Rance?"

"Yessir."

"All right then. Without any modesty or exaggeration, how good are you?"

"Good enough to kill both of them before they can get off a shot," Rance said convincingly.

"Well, I want to do this peacefully, if possible," the sheriff said sternly. "I can tell that woman means a great deal to you. So, are you in complete control of yourself? I want you to shoot only if they refuse to surrender and go for their guns."

"Suits me fine, sheriff. I'll stand to your left, and if they go for their guns, you shoot the man on your right, just in case I can't get them both myself."

"Agreed," Wood said, as they made their way casually but cautiously over to the saloon.

Rance confirmed with a nod that the two men indeed were Raleigh and Madison, who looked up in shock when they recognized Rance even without his fancy show clothes.

Before the sheriff could finish saying, "Surrender peacefully. You're under arrest," the two went for their pistols. One ounce of lead for each of them exploded from Rance's pistol before Raleigh, Madison, or the sheriff could get off a shot.

* * *

Early the next morning, Rance was having breakfast with Sheriff Wood and saying his thanks and goodbyes. Rance had pictures of Raleigh and Madison to take back as proof to Abby, Dr. Percy, and Deputy Clay Hancock. The town's lone professional photographer took a picture of the men lying side by side in their coffins at the undertaker's parlor.

"Well, sheriff, I doubt our paths will cross again, but if you should find yourself in some place my group is performing, I'd like to have you as my guest."

"Appreciate that, Rance. I'd like to see your act. Have to admit though it would take quite a show to impress me more than what I saw you do in the saloon yesterday. You took both of them out before my pistol was even level with the floor.

"You're the best I've ever seen."

Rance heard those words of praise and knew the sheriff meant what he said. What neither Rance nor the sheriff knew at the time is those words would make their way into print, along with a picture the photographer had taken of Rance and Wood standing beside the coffins.

What the subsequent publicity portended for the future—for good or for ill — remained to be seen.

Chapter Twenty-Five

What will the future bring?

On his way back to Albuquerque where Abby was undergoing the long recovery process, Rance's mind was racing with as many thoughts as those that occupied his attention when he was chasing Raleigh and Madison to Rock Lick. Only this time, his mind was on other matters.

Surprisingly, Rance was not plagued with guilt about these shootings the way he was when he killed Kodiak. This time he knew the outlaws. They were not strangers as Kodiak was. This time a dastardly wrong had been done. Unlike the lack of any history of wrongdoing with Kodiak. And just maybe, Rance hoped, killing got easier to deal with after the first one.

Rance was most concerned about Abby, her recovery, and especially her future. What in the world could she do now to enable her to live the independent, unmarried life she had planned? Yes, she had accumulated thirty-some thousand dollars. But even if she lived modestly, that amount would last only about a dozen or so years, and she wasn't even out of her twenties yet.

She had no special education or training. It was most unlikely she and Dr. Percy would get married. They were lovers, true enough; but they were not *in love*. Besides, she did not want to get married, especially out of pity. And if he married at all, his wife would have to be rich and a member of America's monied aristocracy. Otherwise, he would not be happy.

Perhaps Rance could marry Abby. He did love her, but in what ways? As someone he physically desired? As one he admired and whose company he enjoyed? As one he cared so much about, he wanted to take care of her, possibly even save her from eventual poverty?

"Forget that," he told himself. "She has made it abundantly clear she loves me as a friend, but *only* as a friend. And she was as adamant as she could be about that without being ruthless."

With no potential solution reached about Abby's future, Rance turned to his own. After the loss of the Guerreros and the cruel end of Abby's career, Ahiga and Debza would surely be gone by the time he returned to Albuquerque. Of the four acts attracting huge crowds and lots of money a few months ago, only Rance's remained.

Unless Dr. Percy could come up with some suitable substitutes, the Traveling Sharpshooters Exhibition would dissolve. "Then what would I do?" Rance asked himself with dreaded anxiety. "Like Abby, I have no other specific training or education for anything else."

Ranching was out. Farming did not appeal to him. Running a store of some kind would drive him crazy with boredom. Even joining his dad and his brother repairing and selling guns was not a good option because the business was barely busy enough to provide for two families when Tyrone got married in a few months.

Finding no solutions after hours of thought and worry, Rance turned his attention to his aching head. To escape into another world for a little while, he tried to conjure up something on the bright side.

At least, he conceded, it wasn't raining.

* * *

What Rance did not know and had no way of realizing was that forces beyond his knowledge and certainly his control were racing to affect his future and to enrich a few entrepreneurs along the way.

Preston Doddridge, the photographer in Beards Fork, published in the local newspaper the picture of Rance, the sheriff, and the dead men in their coffins. An accompanying story written by the editor, Roane Webster, not only described the shootings but greatly exaggerated every detail, making out the sheriff to be a celebrated hero, and Rance to be the fastest, most deadly shootist in the West.

Knowing they had a photo and a story with wider appeal than just Beards Fork and with considerable potential profit, Webster started copyright proceedings and contacted several big eastern city editors offering the story and photograph for a price. He knew for certain Easterners loved reading about the Wild West, and the editors would quickly agree to make the purchase.

Within a few months, Rance's name was known to an untold number of Americans and Europeans who had an interest in reading about sharpshooters with a fast draw and the fearlessness of facing an equally fearless opponent in a showdown to the death.

Rance had a mixed reaction to all the attention. Dr. Percy did not. The professor might be down to a one-man act, but that man had been celebrated into major star status. How long that might last, Dr. Percy did not know, but while it did, he was going to milk every dollar out of it he could.

Another huge boost to Rance's reputation—whether he wanted it or not—were two of those infamous "Dime Novels" that flooded the East and much of the rest of the country. One featured the two shootouts in Beard's Fork; the other turned Rance's killing of Kodiak into a David versus Goliath tale.

And while Rance's head was still spinning, two other big moneymaking offers came his way. Smith & Wesson offered him five thousand dollars for the right to reproduce and sell a replica of the pistol his father and brother had made for him. Rance would also receive one dollar for each pistol sold, and his father and brother not only would be promoted as the designers of the pistol but also would receive fifty cents apiece for each gun the company sold. And Smith & Wesson expected to sell thousands, especially to collectors all over the world.

Collectors with more money than good sense also wanted to buy the gun and holster Rance had used in both shootings. Rance turned them all down—that is, until one of Dr. Percy's oil-rich friends offered five thousand dollars for it and kept upping the ante until Rance finally gave in at twenty-five thousand dollars, along with a signed photo of him holding the gun.

As Rance would soon discover, these new sources of income could not have come at a better time.

Chapter Twenty-Six

Old successes, new possibilities

The Traveling Sharpshooters Exhibition had come to its end.

Regardless of all the attention Rance had gotten, with only Dr. Percy's sharpshooter left, fairs and shows were no longer willing to give his one-man act first billing or to pay it top money, especially after he removed the challenges from the performance because they had led to three deaths and Abby's mangled hand. Dr. Percy had no luck in trying to replace the three other acts that made the troupe the best in the West, able to perform two mostly different shows a day.

There was no chance the Guerreros would return. Lorenzo made it clear from the beginning, he and his daughter would perform with their handsome, talented horse for only one season. And they did not last that long after receiving orders for a new position from the president of Mexico.

Ahiga and Dezba had returned to their Navajo home with no interest in straying far to perform, especially since their friends, the Guerreros, had left.

Abby's gnarled gun hand was irrevocably ruined. Her fingers were stiff, so her performing days were gone for good. In addition, she turned down proposals of marriage from both Dr. Percy and Rance—not because she thought they were offering out of pity but because she knew both loved her but were not *in love* with her, and she was still determined never to marry again. They wanted to take care of her because they knew once her money ran out in a few years, she had no other way to make a decent living.

Fortunately, the widespread attention about Rance's killing of Abby's two tormentors had one good outcome. News of Rance's fast draw and the deaths of the two scoundrels had been published so widely throughout the country and in some parts of Europe, the father of Annie Oakley heard about it and contacted his cousin, Abby's father.

Informed that Abby would no longer be able to perform, Annie's father had what he hoped would be a solution that included neither pity nor charity. He contacted Abby's father a second time to tell him Annie needed a personal assistant she could trust to keep her prepared for her shows by making certain her costumes were in good condition, but especially because she needed someone with rifle expertise to keep hers in excellent working order.

Who better to fill that position than Abby?

Two days later, Abby received a telegram from Annie, telling her to look for a detailed letter that would arrive as soon as the postal service could get it to her. She made a straightforward offer.

"Dear cousin Abby. I am sorry and more than a little angry to hear about what happened to you. You may not be able to perform any longer, but you still have more knowledge about rifles and shooting competitions than any other woman besides me. My offer for you to be my personal assistant is sincere and has no ulterior motive. Wire me back immediately and give me your answer. I need you. Your loving cousin, Annie."

Trusting that she was truly needed, Abby accepted the offer, took a ship to England and caught up with Annie in London, where she was launching her tour of European capitals.

Dr. Percy, too, had a backup plan. He always did; he was far too intelligent to put his entire future into one venture—even though the Traveling Sharpshooters Exhibition had earned him a great deal of money. That income, plus the one hundred thousand dollars he received from the oil venture, made him a wealthy man. But it was not nearly what he needed to find his place among his oil-rich multimillionaire acquaintances in the West or his aristocratic friends in the East.

However, Dr. Percy had so many more assets than the money he had thus far accumulated. He was willing to marry for money to secure his place in the world in which he wished to live. His assets: He was handsome, relatively young, irresistibly charming, extraordinarily articulate, and held a Ph.D., the highest academic degree anyone could earn. He had a lot to offer a rich man's daughter or even an older widow who was still attractive and had inherited millions.

Rance was both happy and relieved for Abby, and his admiration for Annie rose from appreciation for her shooting skills to include her genuine goodness as a person. As far as Dr. Percy was concerned, Rance was endlessly impressed by his wisdom and amused by his cunning.

The immediate path Rance saw for himself was to go home, enjoy his growing family, do some thinking about his future, and make a thousand dollars for each of the twelve or so trips Smith & Wesson officials wanted him to take throughout the United States and to several places in Europe.

Chapter Twenty-Seven

Maintaining his relationships
Five years later

Rance balances three-year-old Veronica on his right knee and two-year-old Chet on his left as he sits on a swing on the sunny side porch of the stately house he bought for his parents in Mabscott.

Veronica is the melt-your-heart-with-a-smile mischievous daughter of Tyrone, who wed his high school sweetheart, Phoebe Bankenbott, soon after Rance returned to his hometown five years ago. Tyrone is running the family gun repair business with his father, Patterson, who has assumed a secondary role to give him more leisure time to enjoy his grandchildren.

Chet is the too-beautiful-to-be-true son of Taylor, who three years ago married Jackson Barbour, the lawyer who acted as the agent for the sale of the mansion the Cabells now occupy. Apparently while Taylor and the rest of the family were looking over the house when Jackson opened it for them to tour, the young attorney was giving most of his attention to beautiful Taylor.

Taylor's mother, Fanny, was just a year off in her prediction that her daughter's single life would not last long after her sixteenth birthday. She was seventeen when she married Jackson.

Both Tyrone and his wife and Taylor and her husband built houses on the Patterson property, so when Rance returned, he took over the family's former living quarters over the gun shop. It gave him a secure place to store his expensive weapons and his other valuables while he traveled all over the United States and several European capitals to promote the Smith & Wesson pistols.

Rance still practiced regularly to keep his fast draw and shooting skills intact, but he did not form or join any other traveling exhibition. As part of his tour for Smith & Wesson, Rance gave flashy performances for the potential buyers of the special gun named for him. The tours were successful, but Rance knew they would not continue indefinitely. His killing of three men in gun duels was hot news for a time, but like all other topics, it eventually would fade away.

Consequently, Rance put into practice lessons learned from his mentor, Dr. Percy, and determined to emulate his entrepreneurial skills by purchasing several businesses and plots of land in and around Mabscott. Rance had no interest in being a storekeeper, but owning one was a different proposition. So, when the proprietor of the town's only big general supply store decided to retire, Rance bought it and hired a trusted old school friend, Marshall Jefferson, as manager.

Rance also bought the only hotel in town, renamed it The Cabell House, and put Taylor's brother-in-law, Harrison Barbour, in charge. Like his brother Jackson, Harrison was college educated with a degree in business.

Rance's other venture was expanding the hotel's first floor to include a restaurant, both for hotel guests and the public. The idea was not his. His mother, sister, and sister-in-law surprised him with the suggestion. They were all good cooks who could take turns preparing homemade meals without spending too much time away from their primary responsibilities of running their households and taking care of the children.

Because he liked the idea of owning without the obligation of being tied down by the day-to-day workings of his businesses, Rance put Jackson and his law skills and Harrison and his business talents into overseeing everything. All Rance wanted to be bothered with were regular reports and profits.

These investments were about as far ahead as Rance had planned. Mabscott and his family formed his base, but he spent about half of his time traveling, mostly for Smith & Wesson but also because he found he liked moving around and seeing new places.

Before he returned to Mabscott five years ago, his reputation in his hometown was as that nice Cabell kid who had developed sensational skills as an exhibition shooter and was becoming famous throughout the West. His old friends and the townspeople welcomed him back, but their presence around him had changed. It was disappointing but obvious to him they now saw him not only as a star attraction in a show business act but also as a shootist—a man whose fast draw had taken the lives of three others. All three were bad men with evil motives; the citizens of Mabscott had no doubt about that. But Rance nevertheless had taken lives.

The deaths of those men were a forbidden topic to the Cabells. Rance's mother said with finality it was never to be spoken of again. And it wasn't by family members.

Regardless, Rance was not looked upon the same way he was previously. Now he not only was respected and admired but feared. People were noticeably on guard not to offend or anger him. That behavior was unnecessary because Rance would never harm an innocent person, whether he was known to him or a complete stranger.

Although not of his choosing, Rance had gone down a path in life from which there was no return.

* * *

Rance stayed in touch with Dr. Percy and Abby. Each wrote the other two faithfully a couple of times a month. They kept informed about one another's schedules, and that made it possible for them to get together at least once a year when they found themselves simultaneously working in the same cities or close enough to be able to travel short distances to get together.

The men were delighted to find out Abby had settled into a satisfying and interesting lifestyle as Annie's personal assistant.

"Annie has been kind and really considerate," Abby explained. "But better than that, we've become close friends and confidants. We talk about everything, just as sisters would.

"When we're not working, we run around together. You know, I never thought much about traveling around Europe, mainly because I never thought I've have the chance. But I've developed a taste for it. I'm even getting an education," she said seriously.

"Seeing all those beautiful old, old cities and historic places has been awesome.

"Can't you tell how much more sophisticated and worldly I've become?" she laughed.

"And don't get me started on the food. I love eating all those different delicacies, especially while sitting at an outside table of a restaurant and watching people walking by speaking all kinds of languages I don't even recognize. It really has been a fun education.

"But I'm monopolizing the conversation, aren't I? You can tell I'm having the time of my life, can't you? But it's your turn to bring me up to date on what you two have been up to."

"No," Dr. Percy says. "Tell us more. Sounds as if your life has been much more interesting than anything we have to say."

So, Abby reaffirms her lack of interest in marrying, but she reveals she has met some very different men and enjoyed their company as she and Annie moved quickly from one place to another. As she told Rance when she first got to know him, she didn't want a marriage, but she still enjoyed men.

Rance inferred that meant Abby was sexually active, and a pang of jealousy reared its ugly head again. He remembered once asking Abby why she chose Dr. Percy for a lover over him, and now he was finding out she was choosing to have brief affairs with men who were essentially strangers. After all, Rance loved and desired her, and she knew it.

"Why not me?" Rance again asked himself. It hurt, and he resented it. "Guess that's one disappointment I'll carry to my grave."

As for the artfully skillful—and crafty—Dr. Percy, well, he kept landing nimbly on his feet. His oil-rich friends enjoyed his companionship and company so much, they kept alerting him to money-making investments, so he continued to advance closer to acquiring the fortune that remained his life's goal. In addition, his good looks, charm, wit, and intelligence continued to attract the attention of wealthy ladies, both those looking for a suitable husband and a few married ones looking for an amusing fling.

When Abby playfully elbowed him in his ribs and pressed for more details, Dr. Percy admitted he had his eye on an almost sinfully rich widow who appeared to be equally interested in him. She was soaked in oil money left to her by her husband, and she spent lavishly on Dr. Percy.

"Gonna marry her?" Rance laughed.

"Just might. I'll let both of you know, because if I do, I want you there to experience the spectacular wedding I'm sure she will want."

When it became Rance's time to talk about his life, he admitted he still carried a deep love for Antonella, and he was frustrated by being unable to have any contact with her. He asked if either Abby or Dr. Percy had heard any news about the Guerreros. Unfortunately, Rance could not contact her directly, and neither he nor Antonella had found a trusted third party through whom to send messages.

Fortunately for Rance, Abby was in contact. Because she was a woman and presented no romantic threat, Lorenzo and Alexia welcomed her correspondence. However, the information Abby was able to share with Rance was not what he wanted to hear.

As Antonella expected—and dreaded—her parents had her married off within a year of their leaving the tour to return to Mexico City where Lorenzo assumed his new duties. And because his work occasionally made it necessary for him to make personal reports to President Diaz, Lorenzo and his family were frequently invited to official state events.

It was at one such affair where the president's twenty-five-year-old son Diego got his first look at beautiful, desirable Antonella. She soon found herself seated near the head of the table with Diego and immediately disliked him. She thought him repulsive. He was a loud braggart, constantly reminding others how important he was as a member of the country's first family. In addition, he drank too much, ate too much, and apparently did nothing more than live off his father, who assigned him "positions" that required nothing of him.

He dressed in rich, fashionable clothes, but they could not hide his bulk, acquired by his self-indulgent habits and an apparent aversion to any activity that involved exercise. The one positive he had going for him was a face that came close to being handsome.

Abby saved the worst information for last. Antonella was given no choice. Diego spoke to his father. His father spoke to Abby's father. And Abby's father spoke to her. Within weeks of their first meeting, Antonella obediently married Diego, even though she loathed him. Just before their first wedding anniversary, they had a son.

Abby reported that Antonella retaliated against this forced marriage in the only way she could. Because Diego was never in love with her, just in lust with her beautiful face and body, she used her pregnancy as an excuse to gain thirty pounds, which she did not plan to lose. That was her way of chilling Diego's ardor for spending time in bed with her. Antonella said if Diego turned to mistresses, she would be delighted.

Hearing all of this about the young woman with whom he had experienced a sweet, loving surrender of their virginity pushed Rance into a state of agony. He kept his thoughts to himself but felt like vomiting. Instead, he sought some satisfaction by killing Diego in his mind—over and over.

Rance also felt deep resentment for Lorenzo and Alexia, whom he otherwise genuinely admired and liked. He knew they could not refuse the wishes of the president, but he also knew that even if the president had not wanted Antonella to marry his son, the Guerreros still would have "auctioned" her off to some other high positioned man in a match that would be advantageous to the family.

As he entered his late twenties, Rance still had had no lasting luck with the ladies. One woman he loved would not marry him; the other could not.

Chapter Twenty-Eight

Facing reality

Rance figured it was time to face reality. He knew a good deal about what he was not and did not want to be, but he remained stumped about what path he could find happiness following.

Dr. Percy knew, and had known for years, what he wanted: to be filthy rich with his place in life firmly established among the wealthy and the elite.

Ever since Rance had known Abby, she had centered her ambitions on being independently wealthy and single, restricting her relationships with men to those who amused her and satisfied her romantic and sexual needs.

Rance knew only what he *did not* want to be.

One thing Rance did know for sure was that Dr. Percy, with his superficial, self-absorbed ambitions, and Abby, despite having a gnarled hand that ended her sharpshooting career, were both happier than he was.

Those two had their lives mapped out and needed no compass to find their way. Rance didn't know if his future was north, east, south, or west.

He owned a general supply store, a hotel, a restaurant, and a considerable amount of land. But he wouldn't consider for a moment working in them, or farming or raising cattle on them. They simply were sources of income and investments.

Rance could keep thinking and imagining until even his hair hurt, but he could come up with only three things that had ever interested him: guns, females, and bullies. He had succeeded spectacularly at one, had little success so far with another, and had killed three of the latter.

He could continue for a while exhibiting his skills as a sharpshooter. He was not yet about to give up on women. And he still was consumed with the desire to kick the ass of or kill every bully who tried to pick on him as Kodiak had, or to defend anyone else who was not big enough or strong enough or good enough with a gun to defend himself or herself.

Rance thought briefly about becoming a lawman but rejected that possibility because he knew he would spend more time rounding up drunks than protecting citizens. Besides, the yearly pay was less than Smith & Wesson paid him for a three-day exhibition, and the job was dangerous.

Preachers saved lives and souls, but he wasn't cut out for that either.

He had plenty of money and sources for a steady income that should last indefinitely. The Smith & Wesson royalties would keep rolling in as long as the gun named for him remained popular. He did not have to work at anything. But traveling and consorting briefly with willing women throughout the United States and Europe would eventually grow tiresome.

Rance dearly loved his niece and his nephew, and he had as positive examples the successful marriages of his parents and his siblings to demonstrate what a good life being a family man could be. But it also demonstrated that to be a successful spouse and father would require almost all of his time and dedication.

"Wish I wanted that kind of life," he repeatedly told himself. But deep down, he had to admit he did not. At least not yet.

Perhaps Antonella could have given him that kind of future. She was continually in his thoughts, and he knew he would always love her. But that love could not be.

Rance concluded he needed advice from someone who knew him well enough to be able to help him. As much as his parents and siblings loved him and wanted the best for him, Rance knew they would have no suggestions other than the mundane possibilities he already had rejected.

Then it hit him like a bucket full of ice water in the face. "Ask the smartest person you've ever known, you imbecile!" he yelled out loud. "Ask Dr. Percy."

* * *

One of the benefits of maintaining a regular correspondence with Dr. Percy was Rance always knew where he was or was most likely to be. So, in his haste to have advice, Rance sent him a simply worded telegram: *Need your advice. Give thought to what I can best do with my future. Will arrive Thursday afternoon. Rance*

Rance packed immediately, and despite cautioning himself not to get his hopes worked up unreasonably high, he felt excited and confident. He had the same kind of buzz he got from drinking too much spiked punch at a Christmas party. In fact, he had the same kind of anticipation he had felt before opening presents pulled from under the decorated pine tree when he was a boy.

He said his goodbyes to his family—without revealing the real reason for his reunion with Dr. Percy—and boarded the train for Chicago where Dr. Percy and his wealthy widow lady friend were mixing business with pleasure for a couple of weeks.

Traveling at a speed of thirty to forty miles an hour between stops, the train took about two and a half days to reach Chicago. It seemed longer to Rance, who was so eager to get there he had trouble sitting still. He calmed himself by walking miles back and forth from one passenger car to another to pass the time.

Waiting on the platform, dressed as formally and as richly as ever, stood Dr. Percy with a genuine smile of greeting. Standing regally beside him was an extraordinarily attractive middle-aged woman who looked as if she had been constructed and dressed by the best fashion designers, jewelers, and make-up artists in that huge city. She was magnificent. She knew it. And she apparently did not feel the least bit conspicuous because she probably always looked that way. Her name was Isabella Vanoble, and the sight of her lifted Rance's admiration for Dr. Percy to an even higher level.

After a warm greeting between the two men and a proper introduction to Isabella, the three set off in a richly appointed carriage to the ritzy Palmer House restaurant, whose menu choices overwhelmed Rance and whose prices looked like what he might pay for a good horse.

Rance made no attempt to impress Isabella. Dr. Percy knew him well and undoubtedly had already told her everything she needed to know and would be interested in knowing about Dr. Percy's friend and colleague.

Just as Rance had already sized up Isabella and was mightily impressed, she took the measure of him from the train station through dinner. Her first thought was it was unfortunate he was short. She judged him to be nice looking, perhaps even handsome in his own way. Impressive physique, confident in his manliness, perhaps because of his reputation as a fast draw and straight shot who had outperformed everybody he had faced competitively. And for some reason she did not bother to think about, she found it sexually stimulating to be seated with a man who had slain a giant and two no-good outlaws. He may be small, but he definitely is a man's man, she allowed.

A woman with a wealth of experience with men of the West, having lived her entire life in Texas, she felt genuinely surprised that Rance was dangerously exciting.

"I think I'm going to enjoy Rance's company," she said with a wink to Dr. Percy and a flirting smile to Rance.

"Perhaps we'd better order," Dr. Percy said to change the subject.

"So, what looks good to you on the menu, Rance?" he asked.

"Well, seeing as how I don't even know what most of the items are, I think I'll let you surprise me by ordering for me, my friend. You know what I'm used to eating, so pick out something different—as long as it's not snails or something that came off a frog or a pigeon."

That remark gave them all a laugh. Dinner was off to a fun start.

With a couple of suggestions from Isabella, Dr. Percy ordered a multi-course dinner of the catch-of-the-day fish with The Palmer House's famous tartar sauce, oysters on the half shell, beef bourguignon, and a variety of vegetables, cheeses, and fruit. And for dessert, he ordered brownies, a specialty that originated in the Palmer House kitchen.

Rance took one sip of the wine, whose name he could not pronounce, and without comment pushed it aside. He didn't want Isabella to think he had a peasant's palate because all wine tasted to him like vinegar gone flat. He also choked down one raw oyster with a fancy name and found it repulsive. "Like swallowing a gob of snot," he thought but would never be so crude as to use that term in the company of Isabella.

Nevertheless, he was hungry and enjoyed the fish and the beef dishes. He thoroughly loved the brownie and wished he had the recipe to give to his mother for his restaurant in Mabscot.

Isabella and Dr. Percy chatted casually throughout dinner, mostly about places and attractions they wanted to show Rance during the city tour they planned for him.

"We may even go to some of the shadier parts of Chicago, if you brought your pistol along with you in case we run across any hooligans," Isabella teased.

"Never without it," Rance retorted. "Just let me know when we come across anything or anybody you want me to shoot."

"I like your friend, Percy," Isabella said. "I think we're going to have a lot of fun with him before you two have 'The Talk' about his future. Oh, I hope you don't mind that Percy mentioned that to me, Rance. But he had to, or I would have had a tantrum about the two of you slinking off somewhere and ignoring me."

Her large dark eyes sparkled as she jokingly challenged them. Rance was enthralled.

"God Almighty," he almost exclaimed aloud. He wondered what it would be like spending his life around her and women like her. And he just knew from the way Dr. Percy and Isabella seemed so comfortable kidding and flirting with each other that they had been lovers for some time.

"Why not me?" He had asked that question so many times as he tortured himself over his lack of luck with sophisticated ladies.

Chapter Twenty-Nine

Isabella begins her plotting

Rance was not surprised that Dr. Percy had taken his telegram seriously. What did surprise him were the conclusions Dr. Percy had reached and the suggestions he was prepared to discuss.

"You're entirely correct about not being a shopkeeper or remaining a professional sharpshooter for as long as your eyesight and reflexes allowed. And you damned sure wouldn't make much of a preacher," Dr. Percy started, having a good laugh with Rance, who vigorously nodded his head in agreement.

"What you may not know about yourself—but what I am certain of is that you were meant to serve others. To be a protector, if you will. You were bullied as a small child, and that scary experience has defined everything you've chosen to do since then.

"Perhaps because your father is a gunsmith, you would have had a natural interest in weapons. But I doubt your interest would have consumed you to the point that you would want to become a sharpshooter. That's not something one casually becomes. Sharpshooting is rather like an art, like becoming a classical pianist, or an architect designing great structures, or a great writer. Drawing fast and shooting with deadly accuracy requires years of hard work, practice, and an uncompromising devotion.

"Even then, as you know, Rance, most people fall short of these goals. The overwhelming number of people simply become accomplished but not great pianists, architects, and writers. Only a rare few become the best.

"And you, my friend, are one of the best, if not the best. However, being a shootist, even a famous one, has a short life. Oops, pardon me for using such a bad choice of words. Of course, gunmen usually die young. In your case, I'm talking about how long your body will allow you to perform at peak level."

Dr. Percy pauses, giving Rance a chance to voice his opinion. But now that Dr. Percy has told him the future he does not envision for him, Rance is eager to hear what Dr. Percy thinks he can be. Rance says nothing but lifts his arms to chest level and flashes his palms as if to say, "Well, if not those things, then what?"

"You ready to hear this next part, Rance?"

"Hell, yes, Dr. Percy. It's why I've traveled all this way."

"I don't have it all neatly figured out and tied up in a big red ribbon, Rance. But if you want to be an advocate of the people being bullied in one way or another, I think you should consider going into politics or becoming a lawyer or both."

Rance's face exposed his undeniable disappointment. This is not what he expected from Dr. Percy.

"Hear me out, Rance, before you jump to any conclusions. When I say politics, I'm not talking about someone with the ambition to eventually become a member of Congress or president; I'm referring to something like being the mayor of Mabscott or a justice of the peace where you can stand up for every day, ordinary citizens at the local level. Especially those who are illiterate and can't read documents they are asked to sign by landowners, banks, and the like.

"I'm talking about people who have little or no money and can look to you for help. Because of your smart investments, you won't have to charge those who can't pay. Do you see my point so far?"

"Well, yeah. I sure do. I understand how I could be a mayor. I don't need any special qualifications for that. But I don't have the education to be a lawyer. My brother-in-law, Jackson Barbour, went to school for years to become one."

"I'm way ahead of you on that, Rance. You didn't think I'd bring that up without considering all of the possibilities, did you? Rance, you don't have to take law classes in a college to be a lawyer. In the West, most people who practice law became eligible by doing what is called 'reading the law.' It's like an apprenticeship. It's something you could do under the tutelage of Jackson. You learn at your own speed, and when you think you are ready, you take the bar examination. By passing, you have the legal right to open a law office and take on clients."

"How long would that way take to finish?" Rance asked.

"Depends on how much time you are willing to invest. If you give it top priority over all other things you are doing with your life, I would guess a matter of months, considering that you are intelligent, learn fast, and don't have to have a job while you study.

"Whatever you decide, Rance, you know I will help in any way I can. So, give it some thought and let's talk again when you are ready."

"Sounds good, Dr. Percy. Many thanks. You've given me a lot to consider."

* * *

Dr. Percy and Rance meet Isabella for a light lunch in their hotel in downtown Chicago, and then hail a horse-drawn carriage to take Rance to a destination undisclosed to him. Isabella was so fascinated by Rance's talents, she asked Dr. Percy if the city had some big gun dealer with a shooting range. She wanted to see Rance in action.

Dr. Percy told her he was certain Rance would politely decline to make a big show of his shooting abilities. So, she countered—as do most strong-willed women accustomed to getting their way with admiring men—suggesting they "just happen" to walk into such an establishment while sightseeing.

Arguing would be a losing proposition, so Dr. Percy reluctantly agreed. The pretext will be to give Isabella a chance to see the special Smith & Wesson pistol named for Rance. Surely, he would not object to that.

Within the hour, the three are inside the establishment, and Dr. Percy asks to see the special gun. Presuming they are potential buyers, the salesperson asks the usual questions.

"Are you a collector, sir? I ask because this particular model is purchased mostly by weapons experts or more often by aficionados who intend only to put the gun on display."

"We have a unique interest in the Rance Cabell model," Isabella interjects. "May we see it, please?"

"Of course, madam. Please follow me. We have it in a locked display case."

He removes a key from his pocket and puts the gun on the counter.

"Of course, it is not loaded, so feel free to examine it. I would be happy to explain its features, if you like."

"I would like," Isabella responds. "The two gentlemen are already familiar with it."

"Then, sirs, you are aware this gun has what is commonly known as a 'hair trigger' that makes it especially dangerous to handle. If you would like to pull the trigger, you will see what I mean. Also, madam, as these men undoubtedly know, this weapon has perfect balance, and the ivory handle has indentations to reduce the chances it would slip in the hand of the user.

"In the literature Smith & Wesson makes available, it explains that the father of the man for whom the pistol is named created such a handle to prevent slippage during sharpshooting contests or exhibitions. It is one of the company's prized pistols."

"May we put it to the test on your shooting range?" Isabella asks, winking at Dr. Percy and watching Rance's reaction as his suspicions are confirmed. He knew Isabella wanted to see him in action, but he underestimated her ability to pull off such a scheme so slyly.

"Forgive me, please," the salesman sputters, trying to politely find a way to ask if any of the three of them are competent to fire such a weapon. "As I said, this particular gun was designed for collectors. People who actually wear it in the West are shootists, either working for the law or against it."

"Well," Isabella responds confidently, "suppose you talk to your manager, bring the weapon and some ammunition and meet us in a few minutes out back at the shooting range. I assure you we will then put your mind at rest about which one of these men has the qualifications."

As the employee scurries off, Rance gives Isabella a mock rebuking grin and accuses her of devious deception.

"Guilty as charged," she gleefully admits. "Now show me what you've got, Mr. Expert. I've already told Percy I'm thinking about adopting you and taking you home with us," she laughs, as they make their way out the back door.

The manager, a Mr. Helmer, is waiting, the special gun and ammunition in hand.

"Please understand, our reluctance is not meant to be rude. We are only concerned for your safety. Now please tell me about your experience with such weapons."

"Read the name engraved on the pistol, please," Isabella instructs.

"Rance Cabell, madam," he responds.

"Well, Mr. Helmer, the only qualification we need is an introduction," she says, pointing to Rance. "Mr. Helmer, meet Rance Cabell!"

"You're serious!" he gasps. "Of course you are. You wouldn't joke about something like that. An honor to meet you, sir. Please feel free to use my facilities in any way you wish. But may I temporarily close my store and give all my employees the opportunity to watch?"

"Sure," Rance agrees. "May I also use one of your holsters? I prefer to draw and shoot."

Rance adjusts the holster, slips the pistol in and out several times to test the feel of the resistance of the leather. He looks at the metal targets about thirty feet away and twirls the gun to limber his fingers. All the onlookers hold their breath except for Dr. Percy, who knows better than anyone other than Rance what his friend can do. Rance spins, draws with flashing speed, and easily hits every target as fast as he can pull the trigger.

Isabella squeals with delight. The employees shout and applaud.

"Seen enough, Isabella?" he asks.

"No, no, Rance. Do it again. Or better yet, do something harder."

Rance complies, ending with his behind-the-back maneuver that's his biggest crowd pleaser. Rance unbuckles his belt and hands it and the gun back to Mr. Helmer. Ten more minutes pass while Rance satisfies requests for autographs.

"Where to now, Isabella? Still want to take me home with you and Dr. Percy?"

"I'm plotting something devious toward that goal, Rance. I'll let you know when I'm ready. Now, let's go find something else fun to do."

Chapter Thirty

A transformation of sorts for Rance

Like so many other men who throughout the ages have been unwittingly charmed by beautiful, intelligent, and shrewd women, Rance is naively unprepared to deal with Isabella's intentions for his future. She is about to make him her newest plaything or project or both. It's her way of dealing with boredom, a condition she will plot, maneuver, and manipulate with abandon to avoid.

From the moment she learned from Dr. Percy that this young sharpshooter was coming to Chicago to consult with a mentor he trusted to give him insightful, objective advice, Isabella had taken an interest in Rance. Why? She wasn't sure and really didn't care enough to question her motives. She simply was fascinated by a guileless person who had, albeit reluctantly, used his deadly skills to kill three men. Rance might still look boyish, but Isabella had no doubt that only a man confident in his abilities could face fights to the death.

When she tricked Rance into performing at the Chicago gunshop, she became so excited she made up her mind he must return to her home in Branfield, Texas, with her and Dr. Percy. She was going to take his "education" into her own hands and make certain he learned how to function comfortably and confidently in the sophisticated circles of the rich and powerful.

That meant, among other things, learning proper table manners used at five-course dinners and wearing formal clothing he otherwise would loathe. She also wanted to refine his language by purging it of such common colloquialisms as shudda, wudda, goin', wishin', as well as coaching him on how to make casual conversation with upper-class ladies, young and old,

Dr. Percy excelled in all of these skills, but she knew he would have no interest in tutoring Rance in these endeavors. Dr. Percy could teach him how to interact with a variety of wealthy, powerful, influential men, including the honest and the dishonest, the trustful and the devious, the superficial playboys and the tobacco-chewing men who had advanced through hard work, violence, and ruthlessness to reach their state of wealth and power.

As soon as Dr. Percy became aware of Isabella's plotting, he had a precautionary talk with Rance and warned him.

"You need to understand, Rance, that much of what Isabella wants for you will be of enormous benefit to you. But always—and I emphasize *always*—that in addition to sincerely wanting to mold you, she also always has ulterior motives. You are a project on whose behalf she is willing to devote endless hours of planting, pruning, and grooming. But if you ever fail to take her seriously or ever give her the impression you are less than captivated by her beauty and her charm, she will turn on you and strike like a cobra.

"So, I suggest you give her a chance because she is smarter and more capable than all but a few other people you will meet in your life. She can make a real difference. I know her well, and because I am even more perceptive and self-centered in reaching my goals than she is, I get along well with her. To the point that we probably will be married before you eventually return to Mabscott to do the good you want to provide there."

Rance will soon realize Isabella might be an even better judge of people's wants and needs than Dr. Percy. She already has an offer that Rance can't refuse because it will prepare him better for a future in Mabscott than anything else that has occurred to Dr. Percy.

* * *

In their last night in Chicago, Isabella invites Rance to join her for lunch. Rance presumes she means for the invitation to include Dr. Percy.

She does not.

Seated at a secluded table in a nice but less than posh restaurant within walking distance of their hotel, Isabella answers the question written all over Rance's face.

"I did not invite Percy, Rance. I wanted a chance to speak with you alone. I have a proposal I want you to listen to in full without interruption. When I am finished having my say, I will return the courtesy by hearing whatever your reply will be.

"I want you to return with me and Percy to my house in Branfield. It's huge, so you will have plenty of privacy. Your first question of course is why. Candidly, it's because I've taken a personal interest in you. You fascinate me. I enjoy your company. So far, I have judged you to be quiet, almost reserved, polite, and courteous.

"But what most intrigues me is a quality you do not appear to have any idea you possess. Rance, there is an element of danger about you that I find irresistible. I think you are the type of man who would go to almost any length to avoid trouble, especially if it is physical. But I think there also is a point beyond which you had better not be goaded, or your reaction could be deadly.

"How do I know? Percy told me how you were transformed from the passive Rance who keeps himself under control to the enraged Rance so affected by the evil act against Abby that nothing could stop you from concentrating your every effort into finding the two men responsible and eventually killing both of them.

"I want two things from you, Rance. First, I want to get to know you as thoroughly as you will allow me. Second, I want to train, educate, and prepare you to function in the circles of the elite and powerful. A circle into which I was born and into which Percy has made it his life's ambition to fit into.

"You may never choose to live in that world. Personally, I doubt you will. But I want you *to be capable of it.* It would enable you to fit into Antonella's world if you two should ever again have opportunities together."

"Antonella!" Rance can't keep from blurting out, appearing not only to be shocked but also barely able to control his anger that she knows about his love for Antonella.

"Please don't be mad with me or with Percy, who obviously told me when I badgered him for all the personal information I could get about you. I bring that up because that is the best incentive I have for getting you to go home with us and letting me tutor you. Who knows what the future may bring?

"My final attempt at persuasion is this: I know a brilliant lawyer, a former lover I will admit, I can persuade to let you read law with him. Even better, if I ask, he will let you observe him work his cases in and out of the courtroom.

"He is both famous and infamous, a protector of the accused and a feared opponent of prosecutors. I have witnessed him being charming, and I have seen him be ruthless. He rarely, if ever, loses a case, but that has made him so many enemies, he is always attended by a bodyguard. With your unparalleled skills, you could fit that need perfectly in the many hours during your travels on behalf of clients.

"If you will agree to allow me to do all I have proposed, you will leave Texas with the ability to function confidently with anyone you may now think "outranks" you, and you will return to Mabscott where

142

you will pass the bar examination and have the authority to perform all functions of a lawyer.

"Give it some serious thought, Rance. Ask Percy what he would do if he were you. You know he will give you his honest opinion. I never beg, Rance; I would never stoop to that level. But in your case, I urge you to take me up on my offer. Nothing will tie you to Texas. You will be just as free to come and go there as you are now in Chicago, or you are in Mabscott.

"Now, as I promised, I'll sit quietly and hear you out."

"Well, Isabella, I feel so overwhelmed, I don't know quite what to say. First, let me thank you for caring enough about me to make me this offer. It could work out to be the most generous opportunity I've had since Dr. Percy formed the Traveling Sharpshooters Exhibition and made me the star attraction. That radically changed my life. I have a feeling your proposal would be life-changing, too.

"So, I hope you can understand, it's so unexpected, and so perplexing, at least for me, that it's too much for me to hold in my head at one time. I need to think and get back to you before you are scheduled to leave. I cannot give you my answer right now," although he already knew she would get her way.

Chapter Thirty-One

Don't stab the steak

After getting settled in at home, Isabella transforms herself into a tutor, eagerly taking on the challenge of refining Rance into a man indistinguishable from all the other gentlemen with whom women of her aristocratic upbringing associate. Of course, Rance would never be completely indistinguishable from the others because of his special skills that always engender an element of fear. Besides, none of the other men in Isabella's circles were always gentlemen; they just had the knowledge of how to be one when they chose to be.

Isabella had her list of priorities all arranged in order in her mind. First, she judged that table manners should be the easiest to refine. She had observed closely in the meals she had shared with Rance that he had mastered the basics. Dr. Percy had already told her about Rance's mother's refined background, coming from an upper-class family in which children were brought up "properly."

So Rance's first lesson after breakfast on his first morning at Isabella's antebellum-style mansion was to follow her to her huge dining room with the longest table he had ever seen. A servant already had placed the plate and utensils Isabella had requested.

She set the beautiful dinner plate in front of the chair in which Rance was seated and began her instruction.

"Rance, you're already knowledgeable because your mother obviously has taught you about the basics like keeping your elbows off the table, chewing small bites, eating with your mouth closed, and not attempting to talk until you clear your mouth of food.

"I am particularly impressed that you know how to handle a knife and a fork properly, placing your index finger over the stem and holding the knife the same way. I cannot emphasize how important that is.

"I find disgustingly repugnant the habit that even many young women have of gripping the fork with a closed fist as if they were preparing to stab the steak. It makes me shiver to think about how uncouth that is, and how it is an instant giveaway that proper training is lacking in those persons' families."

Rance also had been taught to cut only one bite of meat at a time, then to transfer the fork to the other hand before raising the instrument to his mouth. Isabella said she "abhorred" witnessing someone leaving the fork in the hand used to hold the meat while cutting and then turning it upside down before inserting the food into his or her mouth.

Isabella complimented Rance and praised his mother. However, she identified four additional instructions she deemed necessary.

One was for Rance to pat his lips lightly to keep them free of any residue from the meal instead of vigorously rubbing them; another was to eat more slowly, not only to ensure he savored each bite of extraordinarily well-prepared food, but also to appear relaxed while eating and keeping up a polite conversation at the same time. A third was to tuck in his elbows as tightly as possible to keep from intruding into the space of those dining on each side of him; and the fourth was to learn the placement and uses of all of that "extra" silverware by one's plate at a formal dinner.

Isabella took one utensil at a time and showed where it would be placed in relation to the plate when he sat down at the table. Forks to the left, knife and spoons to the right. The cutting edge of the knife should be turned toward the plate. A dessert spoon or fork would be placed above the plate with the fork turned to the right and the spoon to the left.

"Rance, the order in which the food is served dictates the order in which the utensils are used—starting from the outside and working inward. And please remember—because it is another of those dead giveaways about proper manners—that if soup is served, you spoon *away* from yourself toward the front of the bowl.

"I know that sounds inconvenient and perhaps even silly, but its purpose is to allow any potential droppings to fall back into the bowl instead of on your shirt when the spoon moves back across the bowl to your mouth.

"Got all that, my darling pupil? Isabella asks, placing a light kiss on Rance's forehead.

"Good job, Isabella. So, what's next?"

"Dancing, Rance. Something I love even more than sex," she winks. "So come prepared wearing suitable shoes. Cowboy boots are out of the question."

Isabella figures Rance will catch on quickly. After all, a fast draw, quick shot artist has to be agile, have great reflexes, and superb balance.

Chapter Thirty-Two

Rance turns trickster

How wrong can a woman with usually impeccable judgment be?!

She is shocked to find that on the dance floor, Rance steps as if his legs are locked at the knee, and he cannot move naturally to the beat of the music.

Isabella's disappointment is so evident that Rance somehow finds it amusing. Instead of apologizing for his ineptness, he adds to her exasperation.

"If it makes you feel any better, Isabella, I can square dance with the best of them. Any fiddler and banjo players available after one of your fancy dinners?"

"What do you think?" she counters. "I was so pleased at how well the dinner table lessons went that I was optimistic you'd catch on as fast to everything else. Right now, I'd have to make some excuse for you to disappear before the dancing starts.

"Let's skip the waltz lessons until I can get Percy and two or three others in here to spare me the pain of going through all of this by myself.

"Go change your clothes, Rance, and meet me at the corral. I still can't believe a boy from Kansas hasn't mastered riding a horse before he was ten. Go on before I lose all of my patience with you!

"Go find Percy for me," she orders Mattie Grisham, her personal assistant and piano player. Mattie was hired five years previously, not because she was better qualified than other applicants, but because she was the only one who could play the piano. That qualification alone got her the job. Isabella never passes up a chance to dance, so when she has a male visitor with the skills, she always wants a piano player on hand.

Like Isabella, Dr. Percy was surprised to hear Rance seemed to have no skill at dancing. And it puzzled him for the same reasons as it did her. Rance obviously was well coordinated. His showmanship skills demonstrated that.

"Percy, you and a couple of our married friends are going to have to help me teach Rance at least the basics of The Grand March so he can participate in the opening of the dancing, and the waltz so he can have some appeal to the young ladies. His sharpshooting performance may entertain them, but it won't make their little hearts flutter like an exhilarating waltz."

"Don't fret, Isabella. He'll catch on, I'm sure."

"Hope you're right, Percy. Meanwhile let's get him up on a horse or two and see if he can manage them better than he did his introduction to ballroom dancing."

* * *

Isabella moaned in impatience when Alex, one of her hired hands, had to show Rance how to properly saddle a horse. She thought he could at least do that. And when Rance attempted to mount from the wrong side, she could not restrain a burst of vulgar language that caused Dr. Percy to laugh out loud.

Isabella was not amused.

Even Alex risked chuckling when he saw Rance's butt bounce totally out of rhythm with the movement of the horse. "I hope his balls hurt like hell all night," Isabella whispered to Dr. Percy. "I just know he's going to fall off that damn horse any minute now."

"Let's stick around a little longer and see if he catches on," Dr. Percy insists, even as Rance constantly bobbed and weaved as if he were riding a bucking bronco. Isabella, however, couldn't manage an encouraging smile as Rance clumsily maneuvered the horse over to the fence where they were standing.

"I think I've got it now," he announced proudly. "Wanna see what I can do, Isabella?"

"Can't wait," she snapped sarcastically. "Try not to kill yourself, if you don't mind, Rance. I'm not in the mood to attend a funeral anytime soon."

Grinning like a mischievous five-year-old, Rance shifted his feet in the stirrups, took hold of the reins, kicked the horse with his heels and streaked across the corral so fast he could not possibly stop before he got to the fence. Rance leaned his weight forward, guided his horse over the fence, rode him a quarter of a mile down the pasture and returned perfectly in timing with the horse while letting go of the reins and showing off with his hands sticking straight up.

Rance dismounted agilely before bringing the horse to a stop, took a couple of running steps while still holding onto the saddle horn and gracefully twirled himself back onto the saddle.

He looked thoroughly pleased when he came to a halt in front of Isabella and Dr. Percy.

"You sure as hell better not have been a part of this hoax," she spat out at Dr. Percy.

"Don't look at me," he responded. "I'm as shocked as you are. I had no idea he could ride like that."

"See what a fast learner I am, Isabella?"

"Kiss my ass, Rance Cabell," she shouted. "You thought you'd get under my skin by pulling this stunt, didn't you? Well, fact is, I'm so relieved you are competent at doing something other than shooting a pistol, I'll let this pass. But heed this warning: My girls and I are going to make you wear out your shoe leather until you can do every dance in the book.

"You'll soon learn you cannot get the best of me. No man ever has. No man ever will. And that is a solemn fact."

Chapter Thirty-Three

Buck's ground rules

With table manners checked off her list, horsemanship instruction being unnecessary, and a big challenge in dancing lessons being attended to by a number of friends with more patience than she has, Isabella is ready to introduce Rance to the esteemed lawyer with whom he will read law.

She remained dedicated to improving Rance's language skills but has approached that daunting task by attacking it on several fronts. She, Dr. Percy, and the attorney with whom her "pupil" will be spending most of his time over the next several months all have agreed to discreetly correct every grammatical error they hear Rance make. The obvious goal is to use their collective efforts to make a considerable improvement in less than a year.

Isabella gives Rance a brief description of Braxton "Buck" Hannon, Esq.

"As I told you before, Buck can be polished and smooth in an out of the courtroom. But he also can be as ruthless as a drunken barroom brawler. He will not tolerate losing, even if it means being—shall we say—a little shady in his interpretation of the law and his conduct in the courtroom. Frankly, I think you will be wise to learn all of his ways, regardless of whether you either approve of them or ever choose to use them yourself."

Rance had done enough research to learn the path to becoming an attorney before formal education and law schools would become the norm in the Old West. The candidate would "read law" for an undetermined period under the tutelage of an experienced lawyer. The primary texts for reading were Edward Coke's Institutes of the Lawes of England and William Blackstone's famous Commentaries on the Law of England.

The apprentice usually starts with working up wills and contracts and advancing to researching laws for the tutor attorney. Eventually the candidate would perform more of the work of the professional lawyer. At the end of an apprenticeship, in Kansas and in many other states, the candidate would take an oral examination—characterized as unchallenging—before a panel of attorneys already admitted to the bar. The candidate would need to show general knowledge of the law and exhibit good moral character.

John Marshall, who became Chief Justice of the United States, and Presidents Abraham Lincoln and Andrew Jackson followed essentially the same path to becoming attorneys as Rance was committing to take.

Isabella arranged a meeting with the attorney at his favorite bar near his office in Branfield. Buck wastes no time getting to the point. Tutoring is far from his favorite pastime, so he lays down the law, as it were, immediately.

"Rance, even though we have not met previously, I think we can talk like acquaintances instead of strangers because we both are captivated by and captives under the spell of the indomitable Isabella Vanoble. In her own unique, irresistible, persuasive way, she has told me something of your ambition to be an attorney by reading the law under my tutelage.

"She has handpicked me because I am considered the best defense attorney in the whole damn state. She also knows I have made many enemies, some of them quite dangerous. That's why I do not travel without protection. She judges you to be perfect for the job."

He pauses to laugh out loud and shake his head in a gesture of acceptance.

"One does not say no to Isabella without some dreadful conse-
quence, sooner or later, you know. Or perhaps you do not yet know.

"Rance, if Percy or someone else concerned for your well being
hasn't already warned you about Isabella, let me emphasize she rarely
asks for anything she wants. In this case, she *told me* this was the arrangement you and I are to have. In her typical fashion, she did not ask
for my opinion or my approval."

Rance responds to Buck's laugh with one of his own. "I have indeed
been made aware of the way Isabella, shall we say, functions. But I
assure you I do not want to be a pain in the ass to you. I haven't convinced myself yet that I want to be a lawyer, but as Dr. Percy pointed
out, having a law background would give me the credentials and the
credibility to assist people in my hometown, and maybe elsewhere.
People I think are being taken advantage of for any number of reasons."

"Makes good sense, Rance, as does almost everything else Percy
says. I have deep respect for his intellect and judgment. In fact, I am
quite fond of him. If Isabella is wise, she will marry this man, instead
of just using him for whatever pleasure or gain she can get and then
discarding him. As she did me.

"Don't get me wrong. Isabella and I are still close, and in my own
way, I will always love her. However, resisting Isabella is about as fu-
tile as trying to coax oil out of a dry hole.

"So, if we are going to work together as Isabella dictates, I am set-
ting some ground rules."

"Seems the sensible thing to do," Rance responds. "I'm listening."

"All right, Rance. The first thing you need to know is I am not an
easy person to work with. I am impatient, demanding, and I don't give
a shit who likes me or hates me. I play to win. Always to win. By any
means necessary.

"If cases or court proceedings are not going my way, I can be hateful and withdrawn. If you can't accept that, we cannot work together. On the other hand, I love the law and enjoy talking about it with people interested enough and smart enough to keep up with me. Especially if they have any suggestion or method of operation that can help me.

"I would expect you to be with or near me whenever need be. That will cut seriously into your time for privacy, or to party, or to have any number of our desirable Texas beauties hanging from your arm. But by spending so much time with me in and out of court and traveling to and fro, we will be continually talking and plotting strategy, and that will give you a much better legal education than you would get in law school.

"All of this means I'll will work your ass off during your apprenticeship. I will grill you morning to night with questions I expect you to give accurate answers about from your readings, and from what I have been teaching you. Aside from the law, I promised Isabella to correct your grammar until we have you talking like Percy. Well, maybe not Percy. None of us can talk like that guy! I plan to be finished with you and have you off my hands in less than a year while impressing Isabella with what a good job I did.

"How does it sound to you so far?"

"Good and frank, Buck. But I will need some clarification and to set a few ground rules of my own. First, I will not be your underling. I have an established reputation that I believe entitles me to expect the same level of respect that you expect from me. I will refer to you as Mr. Hannon except when we are alone or among mutual friends. Then I think first names would be appropriate.

"Isabella said that around her, you are kind, considerate, affectionate, and a gentleman. She also said whenever you felt the need, especially when you are facing someone who stands in your way, you are a bully.

"Well, sir. I detest bullies and will not tolerate them. Because of my size, I was bullied in school to the point of humiliation. That was probably my main reason for becoming proficient with guns. Once I became an expert, no one dared mess with me.

"I never intended to shoot anything but targets, but of the three men I have shot to death, one was a giant who thought he was goading a farm boy into a fatal gunfight, and the two others were the bastards who smashed Abby's shooting hand and ruined her career. You are aware of those shootings and the circumstances. That's part of my reputation.

"So, I will always treat you with respect, Buck, if you will make it possible. But I tell you for the record, I will not tolerate being spoken down to or bullied. As a friend, I present that simply as information. When I say that to adversaries, it is a deadly warning.

"Finally, even though I have killed, I am not a killer. As both your pupil and your bodyguard, I will protect your life with mine, if necessary. That's an oath I swear before you now. But I won't kill unless the circumstances are so dire I have no choice.

"Because of my size, I cannot be the kind of bodyguard who protects you with my fists. There are plenty of men who can make mincemeat out of me physically. So, if we are threatened, and someone or several people attempt to attack us bodily, I will do what I have done since elementary school. I will pull back my coat and expose my gun and make it clear I am prepared to use it.

"For people who have heard of me, my reputation should be enough to prevent any action against you. For those who just see me as a rather harmless looking small man, I will gladly give them a demonstration of how easily I can knock their two-hundred-pound asses over with one ounce of death expelled out of the barrel of my pistol."

After a pause, it is clear both Buck and Rance have said their piece and have arrived at an understanding.

They extend their arms and seal the deal with a firm handshake—which in the West is the same thing as pledging their word.

Chapter Thirty-Four

The student learns; the sharpshooter protects
Ten months later

Buck's word is good despite the fact that he is full of contradictions. He insists on good grammar and pronunciation from Rance while feeling free to butcher the King's English whenever it suits his purpose. Rance figures out quickly that Buck can adapt his language to whatever situation he finds himself in. Around educated men and women, Buck speaks perfect English. He is gentle, charming, and entertaining in all social circumstances. Around less educated hard-working folks, he talks the way they do. Rance is amazed at how Buck is so adept in switching from one to the other with the smoothest of transitions.

At the end of most days traveling and working with Buck, Rance finds himself enjoying the challenges and roadblocks with which Buck obstructs his path. Buck is like a crusty old Army veteran training recruits, but Rance has to admit his mentor is one hell of an effective teacher.

In addition to law, Buck demands Rance study American history, some classic literature, and of all things, arithmetic. When Rance questions him about the latter, Buck responds with annoyance: "How the hell do you expect to deal with wills and contracts if you can't be accurate with numbers? Please just do as I say and keep the dumbass questions to yourself. I know what I'm doing; you should realize that by now."

Even in the evening when Rance might expect a break, Buck—especially after he has consumed a few shots of bourbon—could get all fired up about the Constitution and especially the Bill of Rights, which he deemed "the greatest document contributed by the Founding Fathers."

"Rance, always look beyond the mere words, as noble as they are. For example, most people should be aware of the overarching importance of the First Amendment. Without free speech, the other nine could not be honored. Now, we all should already know the First Amendment protects free speech and freedom of religion. But I'd bet my last dollar that no more than ten percent of Americans can name the other two provisions. Can you, Rance?"

"Truthfully, Buck, the only reason I know about the right to peacefully assemble and to petition the government for redress of grievances is because you said I'd 'damn better know them' when you quizzed me on them."

"Well, both of those provisions are important to a lawyer, my boy. You will have clients who, for example, have property the government is trying to take to build a road or some such thing. Sometimes that plan can be stopped if justified, but in any case, you can go to court and try to make certain your client is getting paid what the land is worth.

"As for the right to peaceable assembly, that covers a wide range of things from meeting in church, gathering in your homes to discuss political changes you want, or even getting a crowd together in the streets to chant and carry signs for or against one thing or another."

"But from my reading, Buck, that would not include the right to block streets or entrances to shops or hospitals and things like that, would it?"

"Not usually, but there are exceptions, of course. And that's why lawyers have to be up to date on new laws being passed and previous court cases that can be used as precedents."

Rance also concentrated his studies on some of the other amendments Buck lauded: the second protecting the right to bear arms; the fourth disallowing unreasonable searches of homes or properties without probable cause and the issuing of warrants; and the fifth through the eighth, the ones that affect the everyday workings of a lawyer because they deal directly with vital aspects regarding a person's right to apply for bail and to have a fair and speedy trial, and to be protected from cruel and unusual punishment, among other rights.

Rance applied himself diligently and listened carefully, taking prodigious notes and asking endless questions to gain insight about details and applications.

Among those insights were clues Buck had learned over decades about "reading" a jury, preparing a list of every question to be asked of witnesses, and just as important, questions not to ask them for fear they would backfire. And with the sneakiest of expressions on his face, Buck gave advice about how to maneuver in damaging information he knew the judge would tell the jurors to disregard.

"We all do that, Rance. I mean, how the hell can a juror erase that information from his brain? It works, believe me. You push that one up to the edge of contempt, but don't go over that boundary. That will anger the judge and cause the jury to question your ethics."

Buck also lectured Rance on how to throw suspicion off his client and onto another person, even if you know that other person is not guilty.

"In a criminal trial, all we need is 'reasonable doubt' to either win a case or to get a mistrial if we think we are losing."

There was no doubt whatsoever in Rance's mind that Buck knew the law inside and out and how to apply it. Rance soon came to realize Buck also knew how to bend the law right up to the breaking point.

"You need to know how to work all sides of a case, Rance. And, frankly, I don't give a shit if it makes you or anyone else think less of me."

Ten months into the arrangement in which Buck serves as a tutor in return for Rance's protection, all has been peaceful except for one near fight. Everyone who knows Buck is aware he never travels without protection. They've seen him get too many guilty men off with his somewhat less than ethical approach to his job. And that has earned him enemies, more than a few of whom are dangerous.

But Buck is too fond of whisky and an occasional round of cards to stay out of saloons, and that keeps Rance on the alert whenever they enter one. Rance's experience with that giant bully, Kodiac, is one he relives every time he enters one of those establishments.

Buck feels confident that Rance's armed presence is the reason he has not been physically attacked. As usual, the verbal threats continue, but no one has tried to risk clashing with his sharpshooting protector. Rance knows his reputation has offered protection because his physical presence alone certainly would not. What Rance fears, however, but has not mentioned to Buck is what might happen if some badass stranger thinks Buck has cheated him at cards or has otherwise been insulting with his brash manner of speaking?

Inevitably, just such a scenario occurred not long after Rance replaced Buck's former and much bigger and meaner looking bodyguard.

Rance went on the alert as he stood behind Buck near the end of a card game in which a rough-looking owner of a small horse ranch had lost more than he could afford. Buck, as usual, was the big winner. The man stood and angrily demanded Buck either return his money or go for his gun.

"I wouldn't risk that if I were you, mister," Rance intervened.

"Oh yeah. And just what are you going to do about it, you little sawed-off runt? I'll shoot his ass full of holes and then kick yours all over this barroom. So shut the hell up and butt out!"

Rance has no doubt this big half-drunk rancher can do as he threatened, so he responds the only way he can—by pulling back his coat and exposing his fancy pistol and its specially made holster that any experienced westerner would recognize was fashioned to promote a quick draw.

"Mister," Rance says loudly enough for everyone around to hear. "I don't want to shoot you. So I'm giving you a chance to gather up the money you have left and walk out of the bar with no one getting hurt. I repeat: I will not fight unless you leave me no other choice."

"I think you're bluffing, little man."

"Tell you what," Rance offers. "Put both of your hands on the table where I can see them, and with the bartender's permission, I'll show you why you don't want to leave town in a coffin."

"Bull shit!" the man spits. "You just want to get an unfair drop on me."

"I assure you before all these witnesses, that I am on the level. Besides, don't you realize if I shot you down with your hands on the table, I would hang for it?

"Bartender, place five shot glasses on that shelf on the wall over there, about twenty feet away." The bartender complies.

"Please notice I am saving one bullet that I will put in you, mister, if you make the wrong move."

Rance removes his jacket, flexes his fingers, and with all eyes from twenty or so spectators riveted on him, he draws faster than any of the men have ever witnessed before and shatters all five glasses.

The stranger picks up his money and walks out of the saloon without looking back.

Chapter Thirty-Five

The gunfight

After Buck pronounced him ready, Rance makes preparations to return to Kansas in a few weeks, take what passes for a bar examination, and set up a law office in Mabscott.

One case remains to be completed before Rance and Buck terminate their partnership. Buck is defending a twenty-four-year-old habitual criminal charged with killing an elderly woman during a bank robbery in Dallas.

The case is not a popular one to defend, but Buck is under the order of a judge to serve as the man's attorney. The accused, Ramsey Plymouth, has been in an out of jails and prisons since he was a teenager, and public opinion is overwhelmingly against him, especially by the family of the slain woman, who had the misfortune of entering the bank to cash a check just as three outlaws showed up. Her three sons have publicly announced that "if the law doesn't do the right thing, we will!"

As it turns out, the accused man was not even in Dallas at the time of the robbery, and Buck has witnesses to that effect. And although the jurors have no liking for the defendant, the evidence is overwhelming. Ramsey is found not guilty.

The citizens attending the trial boo loudly, shouting insults at the judge, the jury, but especially Buck, on whom they place most of the blame for the verdict. A larger crowd outside the courthouse is even angrier, having been worked up with liquor and calls for justice by the dead woman's sons.

The sheriff gathers Ramsey, Buck, and Rance and leads them to the back door to avoid the crowd. The plan fails. Anticipating such a maneuver, the three brothers station their friends at the front entrance of the courthouse while they wait in hiding at the back door. They expected all along that if Ramsey beat the charge, the sheriff and his deputy would use that exit to avoid a confrontation with the crowd. However, with guns drawn, the brothers surprise the lawmen, surround them and force them to surrender their weapons.

Reacting quickly, Rance pushes Buck and Ramsey behind their awaiting carriage, but not before all three were shot—Buck in his upper left leg, Ramsey in the chest, and Rance in his left shoulder where the bullet exits cleanly without striking a bone or piercing an artery.

As the brothers move in openly to finish off the wounded, Rance draws with his usual flashing speed and with his deadly aim kills two of the brothers, hitting one in the heart and the other in his forehead. The third brother yells, "Don't shoot, don't shoot!" throws down his pistol and raises his hands.

Witnessing what Rance has managed to do in a matter of seconds and seeing that the sheriff and the deputy have reclaimed their weapons, members of the crowd that have run to the back of the courthouse lose their nerve, and the fight is over.

Neither Buck's wound nor Rance's is life-threatening, and they get quick medical treatment at a local doctor's office just down the street. Buck wins his case but loses his client. The shot to his chest is fatal.

The brothers have their vengeance, but the cost is far more than they had expected to pay. The mother and two of her sons are dead, and the one who surrendered is facing either a long jail term or death by hanging.

Buck recovers at his home and Rance at Isabella's. The next time they see each other is at the grandiose wedding of Percy and Isabella.

Chapter Thirty-Six

Dr. Percy delivers revealing news

Dr. Percy and Isabella were both alarmed to hear of Rance's bullet wound and anxiously prepare everything and every caregiver he may need. Dr. Percy is quite anxious about Rance's condition. As is Isabella, but she also is secretly and inexplicably aroused by Rance's ability to face death again and prevail by killing two more men. In her mind it is so savagely brave and primitive.

She can't help making physical contact with him, kissing his cheek and putting her hand on his bandages. "How can it be possible," she asks herself, "that such a boyish, innocent looking young man has thus far prevailed over five bigger men intent on killing him?"

She didn't attempt to reason why such things aroused her. Isabella, as usual, just accepted and somehow enjoyed them and moved on to whatever else she might find worth her time.

When Isabella left, Rance and Dr. Percy had their first chance to talk intimately, as only true friends can do comfortably and confidentially.

"All right, Dr. Percy, "you know I'm bursting to know how this wedding came about. I mean, I knew you would never marry a poor woman. No offense."

"None taken, Rance. Go on with what you were saying."

"Did you propose or did she? What prompted one of you to take the big step?"

"A couple of weeks ago, I told her in one of our more passionate circumstances that I loved her and could not imagine a life without her.

Apparently, she had been biding her time until she could conclude for certain that I truly loved her.

"She knows all about the ambitions that have driven me since I left teaching at the university. You know I haven't kept those motivations a secret from you or Abby or anybody else, including Isabella. But she has been extraordinarily wealthy all of her life. She takes it for granted and presumes everyone else would love the lifestyle as much as she does. She doesn't care one whit that I would not marry her if she were not wealthy."

"So, when's the big day?"

"In a month. We were waiting to hear from Abby. Isabella understands why I want Abby here, just as I would work a date around your presence if it were necessary. You know you two are family to me. We've been through a lot together, mostly good, of course. Our Traveling Sharpshooters Exhibition will always be among my fondest memories—and without question my greatest achievement."

"What kind of a wedding do you think Isabella is planning, Dr. Percy? Any chance she might want to scale it down, considering she was married before for a long, long time?"

"You must be fantasizing, Rance," Dr. Percy laughed. "Haven't you gotten to know Isabella well enough by now to realize she never denies herself any opportunity to put herself on display in all of her finery before an admiring public?

"She can afford the best wedding anyone can imagine, and I guarantee you she will have it. Rance, Isabella has so much oil property, you could take a dinner fork, stab the earth on any of her thousands of acres, and four geysers of black gold would gush ten feet high.

"No, she will have a wedding people will remember the rest of their lives. She told me she is breaking with tradition in any aspect that pleases her. That's so typical of Isabella. She's going to wear a stunning white Parisian gown so loaded with precious gemstones sewn into it that it may double her own weight," he said with an indulgent grin.

"And she will have a small army of attendants to give her best friends a chance to show off, too.

"My friend, you do not have to be a genius to understand Isabella's motives, and besides, she also characteristically doesn't care what anyone else thinks.

"She knows white is supposed to represent sexual purity and all that. But she has witnessed a few of her friends organize what they call a 'reaffirming of their wedding vows' by staging a second wedding and wearing a white gown with a long train that costs a small fortune. The whole thing is usually between a man and a woman who had a modest wedding when they had little money. Now they are oil rich, and by damn she feels cheated.

"Those women aren't the least bit interested in reaffirming their wedding vows. If they were, they would wear church clothes and have a simple ceremony with only family and close friends in attendance. They want a spectacular show in all the finery the best gown designers and wedding planners can provide. And they want everybody who's anybody to be there to see them. The husband is just filling in space at the altar.

Dr. Percy and Rance share a good laugh, knowing, as all men finally come to realize, just how useless it is to waste any more of their time trying to figure out why God made males and females so different.

"The reception will be fabulous and the food sumptuous, too. So don't eat much beforehand. You'll want to come hungry because you'll probably never witness anything else quite like it in your lifetime."

"My small-town mind can't imagine such a celebration, Dr. Percy. But what about you? I've never known you to just fade into the shadows. You know you're a born showman. I'd bet my bottom dollar you've figured out some way to shine, too."

"You know me too well, my friend. Yes, I'll be on display in a long tailcoat with the traditional white shirt and shiny black patent leather slip-ons. But I'll break with custom and wear a bright cranberry colored cummerbund, bow tie, and pocket square with three corners poking out of the top."

Taking advantage of Rance's open-mouth expression, Dr. Percy delivers the crowning touch: "My shirt studs will be solitaire diamonds!"

Rance shakes his head sideways and grins in stunned amazement.

"You're not joking are you, Dr. Percy?"

"Hell no! Men have vanity, too. Why should the bride get all of the attention?"

Chapter Thirty-Seven

Rance brings Abby up to date

Abby arrived from Europe late Thursday before the Saturday afternoon ceremony, giving her enough time to attend the pre-wedding dinner the next day. She and Rance have corresponded and plan to have dinner alone the first evening to give them privacy to talk with just each other. Abby has teased that she has some news or gossip; she's not certain how to characterize it. And she has requested Rance make sure she is seated beside him at the Friday dinner.

It has been more than a year since they last met, breaking a pledge they made not to let that much time ever separate them. But she has been on another European tour with Annie that kept her overseas for fifteen months.

"You look great," they both say at the same time, breaking into laughter at how unoriginal each of them sounded. "No, I truly mean it, Rance. You are aging well. There's no 'boy' there in your face any longer."

"And you still look as delicious as ever, Abby," he replies. "Travel seems to suit you, and I imagine you are totally refined after rubbing shoulders with royalty and maybe adding some sophisticated European language to your vocabulary."

"Oh, yeah. Right. Truth is, Annie is the one invited into those lofty circles. But I have gotten within seeing distance of kings and queens and other members of the nobility. Add that to all of the great sites in so many old, old cities with their museums and galleries and monuments, and I have gotten an education I never dreamed would be possible.

An Ounce of Death

"But so much for me. Tell me at what point you are in the double educations you are getting from Isabella and what's-his-name, the man who's preparing you to become an attorney?"

"Well, Isabella has done her best to make a gentleman out of a Mabscott, Kansas, hayseed. Honestly, she has worked hard, and I have made progress. She's still working on my grammar and pronunciations, but I'm afraid I've been a big disappointment in improving my dancing skills. She hates that because she dearly loves dancing. Truth is, I'm good enough not to embarrass her or myself this weekend.

"You know, I never had reason to ask before, but are you much of a dancer, Abby?"

"I'm good. Well, maybe, even better than that. You'll find out pretty soon. I'm counting on you not to leave me standing on the sidelines alone, going unasked by Isabella's highfalutin friends."

"Don't worry about that, Abby. The way you look, all the men from the youngest to the oldest will be after you. I promise."

The two take a few seconds of silence to enjoy just looking at each other. The moment gives Rance an opportunity to bring up a subject at the forefront of his mind.

"Abby, I know this is an abrupt change of subjects, but I've been itching to know what that news or gossip is you wrote me you knew about. What is it?"

"Rance, I know we both are catching the same train East a few hours after the wedding, so let's wait until then. It will give us something to look forward to. All right?"

"Guess it will have to be. I know you too well to think I can squeeze it out of you before then."

"You're so right about that, Rance. Now, I'm the one who's so curious about this wedding of our Percy to this woman, Isabella. And let me fully admit, I'm just downright nosy about some things.

"Obviously, Percy would not be getting married unless he had found a very rich, beautiful woman he considered interesting enough to spend most of his time around.

"So, just how rich is she, Rance?"

"I don't know the exact figures, Abby, but she has thousands of acres of oil-rich land and loves spending money. I've learned she was born rich and married even richer. So, I suppose it would be accurate to say she has the kind of money that will never run out."

"All right, now tell me what she is like. Describe her to me. Not just how she looks, but how she acts. How she carries herself. Whether she is nice, fun to be around, or whether she is a spoiled, intimidating bitch who rolls over anybody and everybody who gets in her way."

Rance can't answer for laughing until his eyes water. "Damn, Abby, you are nosy. Well, you will know from the first moment you meet her that she is extraordinary in just about every way. She is truly beautiful. She always is totally put together. I mean she is always properly made up, dressed to the extreme, and loves putting herself on display.

"I think the main thing that impresses me is her self-confidence. She is remarkably intuitive (that's a word Dr. Percy taught me). She can size up individuals almost instantly, and that gives her an advantage in dealing with people of every level from her servants to her friends, as well as the business people she has to work with.

"And she can manipulate you in such a way that you don't know what she is planning or scheming until it's a *fait accompli* (that's another French term Dr. Percy has taught me). Obviously, I'm showing off for you. It means that by the time a person realizes Isabella is scheming against you, it is already an accomplished fact. It's also my way of telling you Isabella gets her way not by pouting or throwing a fit, but by outsmarting and outmaneuvering people.

"Both Dr. Percy and Buck Hannon warned me that Isabella always has ulterior motives no matter how nice a thing she does for you."

"Then Percy has her figured out. He knows what he's letting himself in for."

"He does indeed, Abby. I think you and I agree he's the smartest man we've ever known. But I've learned in my years of frustration trying to figure out women that no man—not even one as intelligent as Dr. Percy—can always know what's going on in any woman's mind."

"That's sounds insulting, Rance."

"Nope, just a truth men have to learn to live with."

Rance and Abby paused to let all of this information organize itself in their minds. Then Abby, who also has intelligence and intuition, as well as a genuine love for both Percy and Rance, asks the most important question.

"Do you think Percy and Isabella will be happy together? I mean, truly happy?"

"I've asked myself that question many times since I first met her in Chicago about a year ago, and I have concluded they will."

"And what makes you think so, Rance? Seriously? Honestly, I'm concerned about them."

"I don't think you have to be, Abby. I think they will be happy because they are both honest. Neither makes any effort at all to hide what they want out of life and the motivations behind that.

"She knows her being wealthy is a must. He knows she wants to be married while she is still a stunning beauty in her middle years, which means she can't count on having that quality for many more years.

"She also wants a husband she can show off to her world. Dr. Percy has what she wants. He obviously is tall and handsome, and as smart as anyone she will ever meet. He is *Dr. Percy Merryweather Livingston Hardcastle IV,* which sound more like a title than a name. He can talk at any level with any class of people, and he has enough control over his sizable ego to always let her have the lion's share of the limelight.

"That's why I think they will make a go of their marriage."

"Thank you, Rance. That puts my mind a little more at ease. I guess I'm just extra skeptical because my only experience with marriage was a bad one."

"Then we will see, Abby."

"Yes, Rance. That we will."

Chapter Thirty-Eight

The Wedding

If Rance and Abby thought the previous evening's wedding dinner was the most ostentatious display of wealth they had ever seen, then they were totally unprepared for the ceremony they would soon witness.

To say it was unconventional would be an extreme understatement. Isabella dismissed every custom and every tradition that stood between her and her dreams of a special day to make herself the focus of *all* attention.

First, she must have purchased all the white flowers from every shop in Texas. They were placed everywhere imaginable, and they were spectacular in following her white and green color theme: roses, lilies, jasmine, chrysanthemums, orchids, baby's breath, and a number of other varieties neither Abby nor Rance could identify. The combination, however, blended beautifully. No one could deny that.

Green and white streamers hung in intricate patterns from the ceiling of her cavernous ballroom. Green and white wrist corsages were provided for all the ladies, and the same colors in boutonnieres for the men.

Anyone with severe allergies to flowers would have died on the spot.

Second, Isabella decreed she would walk down the aisle unescorted. Her father was long deceased, and she had no brothers. Neither of her two living uncles were mobile enough to do the job properly. Even if Isabella had someone appropriate available, she had no desire to share the spotlight with anyone else.

She had no bridesmaids because she was not close to any unmarried young women. She chose instead a dozen of her favorite middle-aged friends to serve as matrons of honor. But they were not given the honor of preceding her down the aisle. They were positioned on the side of the minister where Isabella would stand, and Percy's groomsmen (handpicked by Isabella) were on the groom's side. Abby and Rance were honored to be among those chosen.

Third, Isabella selected Buck Hannon to serve as best man, not just because someone had to hand Percy the ring to place on Isabella's finger, but mostly because she wanted Buck and his booming courtroom voice to announce there would be no receiving line immediately after the service. Guests were to proceed directly to the ballroom where Buck would offer a toast and explain the unusual way Isabella preferred for her and Percy to greet everyone individually.

Isabella and a team of wedding dress designers created a cream-colored silk and satin gown with an abundance of hand-placed Honiton lace chosen for its ornate motifs and complex patterns. Beading consisted of emeralds and diamonds of varying sizes. Isabella chose to forego wearing a veil because it would detract from her beautiful hair and face. She focused instead on a tastefully small tiara with fine emeralds and diamonds. Her train was ten feet long and as ornate and impressive as her gown. Her cascading bridal bouquet was made of white roses and baby's breath.

The overall effect was mesmerizing.

If there was a single ounce of shyness or concern for who might think her overall appearance to be outrageously excessive, it didn't show on Isabella's face. She maintained a wide engaging smile that might as well have been saying, "Don't I look absolutely magnificent?" Her expression did not change until she reached her position on the minister's right.

Isabella looked like every female's fantasy vision of a bride, and she knew it, reveling in each moment of the ceremony. No queen could have pulled it off more majestically.

Percy beamed proudly. He loved Isabella's ability to experience joy to its fullest.

When it came time for him to put the wedding ring on Isabella's finger, Percy playfully attempted to momentarily steal the spotlight by opening his coat to display his extravagant row of large solitaire diamond shirt studs. Isabella's old friends chuckled quietly, showing their approval of Percy's attempt to have his one moment of glory.

With an amused smile of his own, the minister repeated his instructions for the groom to place the ring on the bride's finger. Percy did not have the ring, of course. Producing it was the job of the best man. With a flourish of his own, Buck revealed a flawless diamond so large and sparkly that if it had been any bigger, it would have looked vulgar.

Isabella's deep-dimpled smile validated her approval of her own choice of a ring, and with a determination not to be overshadowed even for a minute by anyone including the groom, she reached over and placed her conspicuous ring beside one of Percy's shirt studs, overwhelming it to the point it would have blushed in embarrassment if an inanimate object had the ability to feel shame.

Percy acknowledged his defeat with a chuckle and a shaking of his head sideways, as did everyone else who was not the least surprised that Isabella, as always, got the last laugh.

There was one convention Isabella did honor. She took Percy's arm and walked proudly beside him down the aisle, giving everyone a close-up view of her trophy husband.

But convention ended there. When chairs were resettled to the sides of the ballroom, the orchestra played a few notes to call everyone to attention. Buck offered a toast, followed by the clinking of a few hundred glass flutes filled with fine champagne. Buck encouraged guests to drink up and enjoy all the delicacies created by a staff of pastry chefs because dancing would start immediately. And last until the musicians begged for mercy.

"As you know, our Isabella loves dancing above everything else. So, her individual greeting and expression of appreciation for your presence will be to dance at least a few seconds with every man and boy present. Percy will do the same with all the women and girls.

"Feel free to depart when you have enjoyed about all of the drinks, food and dancing you can stand. For those of you with the energy, Isabella assures me she will be the last one standing on the dance floor, so she also has given me the authority to issue you a dare to wear her out if you can."

The one thing Buck did not have to announce because Isabella had already informed Rance earlier was that "Percy will lead off the dancing with me, but you will be second, Rance. And you better make me look good because I've bragged endlessly that I taught you everything you know.

"So, you and Abby come onto the dance floor at my signal, and we will change partners with all eyes focused on us."

"You're serious, Isabella?"

"Damned right, darling. You and Abby are joining me in dancing to the very end. You know me, Rance; I always extract a price for anything I do for someone." She kissed him lightly on the lips and whispered: "It's payback time."

Chapter Thirty-Nine

Abby has news about Antonella

Rance let only a few minutes lapse after the train pulled away from the station at Branfield before he turned to Abby and asked: "What's the news you said you would tell me when we were alone and headed East? The look on your face was one I've never seen before, but you hid your emotions so well I couldn't tell whether the news was bad or good. I presumed it wasn't urgent, or you wouldn't have held off so long?"

"My, Rance. you are in a rush to know, aren't you? I thought we could talk about that extraordinary wedding first. You do realize you and I will never, ever witness anything like that spectacle again, don't you?"

"Yeah, I mean, it was weirdly wonderful and all that, but let's hear your news first."

"Well, my dear Rance, it concerns Antonella. As you know, she and I have kept up a correspondence since she returned to Mexico. We write about the usual stuff—our health, our travels, the latest in clothes and makeup. Just the usual.

"But occasionally, I can tell she needs a trusted friend to lend a sympathetic ear or to serve as a sounding board or to tell intimate things she would reveal to no one else. Her troubles always center on her marriage. In brief, she hates it. She did not want to marry Diego, as you already know. And she got pregnant so soon after marrying that disgusting sloth that she purposely gained thirty pounds in an effort to become physically undesirable to him.

"Apparently it worked because she said he hasn't lived with her for a long time and pays little or no attention to their son. Fortunately,

Antonella has a strong relationship with the child's grandfather, Diego's dad, the president. She said he adores the child, whose name is Dante, and spends as much time with him as he can.

"Of course, I cannot bring any of this up in my letters to her because of the danger that Diego or a servant or whoever else might read one of them and make the information known to someone who would bring harm to Antonella. Anyway, she said the president has put up with all of Diego's hedonistic lifestyle he is going to tolerate. The president said to teach Diego a lesson, he plans to ship him off to some far distant minor embassy in a country Diego will hate.

"Better still, Antonella's father-in-law has so much respect and concern for her that he has implied he just might find a way to separate her and Diego permanently. She said he has provided no details, and she doesn't know whether that means he approves of her living apart from Diego indefinitely or what. So far, he has not done much more than hint at what he might do. If the president chose to, he probably has the influence to pressure the Catholic church to approve an annulment of their marriage. As you know, an outright divorce in the Catholic church is out of the question."

"Are you saying that's simply a possibility or is a realistic expectation for Antonella?" Rance asks in what he hopes is a calm voice although his heart is beating too fast for someone sitting still.

"Beats the hell out of me, Rance. All we can do is wish things work for whatever is in Antonella's best interest. Without the president's support, she absolutely cannot run away and leave Diego without ruining her family's standing within the government and in their social class. And probably their wealth on top of that. Antonella, you know, would sacrifice her happiness to keep that from happening. In fact, that's exactly what she did when she married the president's son!"

"Wish I could either write her or go to see her," Rance blurts out.

"Oh, no, Rance. I know why you feel that way, but I warn you in the strongest terms not to do that. It would certainly lead to a disastrous outcome for Antonella and her family. I give you my word I will relay to you anything I hear from Antonella that sheds any more light on her situation. You have my solemn promise."

"You're right, of course, Abby. It's just so damn frustrating not to be able to do anything to help her."

"Are you saying you are still romantically interested in her, my friend?"

I don't know what I am, Abby. I honestly do not know."

Chapter Forty

A search for happiness

Rance felt overtaken by loneliness and uncertainty after they changed trains for Abby to head North to Chicago and for him to continue East and northward to Mabscott.

The feeling was familiar. He had experienced it several times when he was making the transition between the life he had been living and the one he was moving on to. It made him wonder if people actually lived several lifetimes divided into blocks of years.

For Rance, the first block was his comfortable, safe, and mostly carefree years growing up in a small town under the loving care of wonderful parents and the constant company of two siblings, a bunch of friends he saw almost every day, a church he attended Wednesdays and Sundays, and schools he went to Monday through Friday.

That was life number one, which during his high school years expanded to include frequent travel to compete in shooting matches for sometimes days at a time. But his father was always with him, and they always returned home to all the familiar people and things that made him feel safe and protected.

The transition to life number two with Dr. Percy and the building of the Traveling Sharpshooters Exhibition was much more difficult because it was almost totally different. Although he always had his folks at home to return to if he couldn't endure the change, he was truly on his own for the first time. Not even his father was with him to make arrangements, give advice, and take care of him.

The emptiness made him doubt himself, his choices, and his abilities. But as the weeks went by, he fit himself into a routine that felt natural, and he adjusted. He quickly came to appreciate the excitement and the exhilaration of performing. He loved the admiration of the crowds. He also learned what it was like to be infatuated with a woman who liked him and was kind to him, but who treated him like a boy she was years ahead of in experience and sophistication.

Life number three came when his troupe fell apart after losing the Guerreros, Ahiga and Dezba, and Abby. That's also when Rance met the incomparable Isabella and at her insistence was placed under her tutelage and Buck's. Once again, Rance found himself in an unfamiliar place surrounded by people he did not know.

Now as he rode the train alone, very much missing Abby, Dr. Percy, Isabella, and even Buck, who had worked him so hard, Rance was moving into life number four, and all the uncertainty and fear of the future landed heavily on him again.

Shouldn't going back home to Mabscott to live be something more appropriate when he retired? Not when he was in his twenties, even though he could probably pull it off financially.

He had income from the hotel, the general store, the restaurant, and he had leased his many acres of property near the town to farmers and ranchers. He also was still traveling for Smith & Wesson, making one thousand dollars plus expenses for each talk and exhibition in major cities in the U.S. and in Europe. Not to mention the nearly fifty thousand dollars he had in savings.

Nevertheless, he envied Dr. Percy and Abby, both of whom seemed much happier with their lifestyle choices than he was with his. Dr. Percy at long last had married into great wealth with a beautiful, interesting woman, fulfilling goals he set years ago. And Abby seemed content to remain independent while sampling among American and European beaus who satisfied her romantic and sexual needs.

Rance would have gladly married either Abby or Antonella. But Abby loved him like a brother, and Antonella was a captive in a marriage with a man she detested but could not leave without ruining her family.

When he thought of his prospects for marriage in Mabscott, Rance could see no hope there. Women his age were already married and had children. The younger women were as many years behind him in experience and sophistication as he was when he first met Abby.

The positives for moving back to Mabscott were first and foremost being with his mother and father and his siblings and their families. Sharing Sunday dinners at his parents' home, being with loved ones at Easter, Thanksgiving, and Christmas. Celebrating birthdays, anniversaries, and enjoying his role of a doting uncle.

In addition, he would still be traveling to major cities in America and in Europe for Smith & Wesson as long as the pistol named for him remained popular and profitable. And he had the money to travel whenever and wherever he wanted.

Most of all, apart from his family, he would be building a law practice for which Buck had educated him as thoroughly as possible. He could start helping those who needed him the most. That alone should make his life feel worthwhile.

Stage four also had one other advantage. He knew the people and the town to which he was returning. When he joined Dr. Percy, he knew no one. He no longer saw anyone who had been part of his everyday life. When he went to live in Isabella's mansion, he knew only Dr. Percy and had just met Isabella. He no longer saw Abby, the Guerreros, or Ahiga and Dezba.

As empty, as lonely, and as conflicted as he felt making that train ride, Rance couldn't wait to get home. He had little choice in making the transition. Abby and Dr. Percy had their own lives to live. Antonella was untouchable. So, home it was. And the sooner the better.

* * *

Because Rance had informed his family of the approximate date of his return, they had not sent him his mail for almost a month. Weary after his six-hundred-mile trip from Branfield, Rance plopped down onto the comfortable reading chair he has used so often it has molded itself to the shape of his body.

As he gave each piece of mail a cursory glance to see what interested him, the sender's address on one envelope jolted him upright. It is from Antonella, the only direct communication between them since her family left the Traveling Sharpshooters Exhibition years ago.

The message was simple and to the point:

"Dearest Rance, you once told me I could come to you at any point in our lives, regardless of whether you are still single or have a wife and a bunch of children. Well, that time is now. I am free of Diego and have the blessing of my parents to be with you.

"I do not want to travel alone with my son. So, if you still want me, come and get me."

Rance dropped all the other envelopes as he stood and walked to his bed where his suitcase lay open, full of clean clothing ready to be unloaded and put away.

He closed the lid, locked the luggage, and placed it by his front door.

About the Author

George T. Arnold, Ph.D., is a professor emeritus in the W. Page Pitt School of Journalism and Mass Communications at Marshall University where he taught news and feature writing, language skills, ethics, and media law for 36 years. He worked full-time for seven years as a newspaper reporter to finance bachelor's and master's degrees from Marshall, and he has a doctorate in journalism and mass communications from Ohio University.

His textbook/resource book, *Media Writer's Handbook, a Guide to Common Writing and Editing Problems*, is in its seventh edition and third decade of continuous publication. It has been purchased at more than 300 colleges and universities in the United States and abroad. It won the Gold Medal first-place award in the 2021 Readers' Favorite International Book Awards, nonfiction/education division.

Dr. Arnold is the author of more than 50 professional and academic articles, several short stories and has had four novels published by Speaking Volumes: *Wyandotte Bound, Old Mrs. Kimble's Mansion, The Heart Beneath the Badge, and An Ounce of Death.*

Wyandotte Bound won the Laramie Award first place for Best Western in the 2021 Chanticleer International Book Award competition and was a winner in the 2024 International Impact Book Awards in the Traditional Fiction category.

Old Mrs. Kimble's Mansion was a winner in the 2024 International Impact Book Awards competition in the Relationships category.

The Heart Beneath the Badge won one of the most prestigious awards in American literature: the Western Writers of America's Spur Award for Best Western Romance novel published in 2023. It also was a winner in the 2024 International Impact Book Awards in the Romance category.

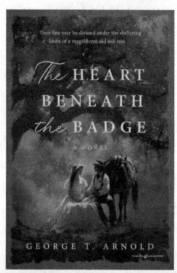

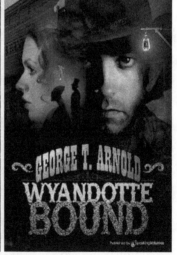

Now Available!

AWARD-WINNING AUTHOR
ROBERT J. RANDISI
The Sons of Daniel Shaye

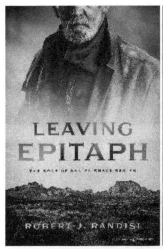
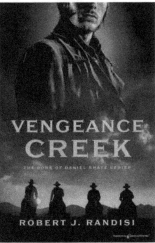
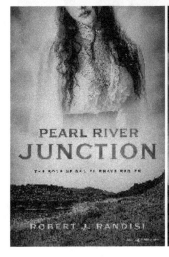
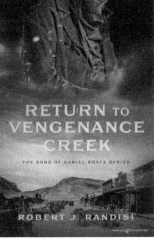

**For more information
visit: www.SpeakingVolumes.us**

  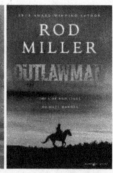 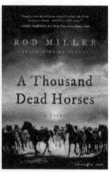
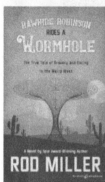  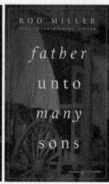 

Now Available!

SPUR AWARD-WINNING AUTHOR
JOHN D. NESBITT

Action / Adventure Westerns

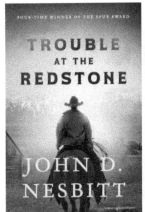
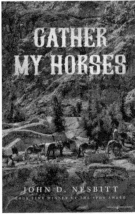
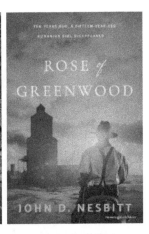

For more information
visit: www.SpeakingVolumes.us